There was more to Da

And it was only the fact that she hated losing and wanted her boss to think she was the best that made her fight the attraction she felt toward the senator.

She wasn't about to do something driven by hormones and ruin her hard work. She was young and had her entire career in front of her, and he was just a guy. A hot, sexy man who she needed to figure out so she could best him when they were both back in DC.

She just hoped she could remember that.

He lifted his champagne flute in a toast.

"To wedding crashers."

"To wedding bouncers," she replied.

He threw his head back and laughed, which set off butterflies in her stomach, making her realize that Dare Bisset was already becoming much more than just a work goal she was determined to achieve.

* * *

Secrets of a Wedding Crasher
by Katherine Garbera is part of the
Destination Wedding series.

Dear Reader,

I'm both excited and a little sad to bring you the last book in the Destination Wedding series. I have enjoyed all the twists and turns the Bisset and Williams families have taken and hope you have, too. Of course, it's not over yet!

Dare honestly is one of my favorite characters I've ever written; he's a little bit me as the eldest child. He's the peacemaker in his family, but he still has those same passions that they do. He just always tries to keep his image clean, which works pretty well until Melody crashes his cousin's wedding.

Melody is also me in my twenties. There was nothing I didn't want and couldn't achieve. Sometimes, though, I made missteps—who doesn't, right? She's so young and eager to prove herself. She takes a chance, not expecting to actually like Dare or wind up in his bed.

And right now the last thing that Dare wants is another scandal!

Happy reading!

Katherine Garbera

KATHERINE GARBERA

SECRETS OF A WEDDING CRASHER

HARLEQUIN®
DESIRE™

Recycling programs
for this product may
not exist in your area.

ISBN-13: 978-1-335-73563-8

Secrets of a Wedding Crasher

Harlequin Enterprises ULC
22 Adelaide St. West, 41st Floor
Toronto, Ontario M5H 4E3, Canada
www.Harlequin.com

Printed in U.S.A.

Katherine Garbera is the *USA TODAY* bestselling author of more than 120 books. She started her career twenty-five years ago at Harlequin Desire writing about strong alpha heroes and feisty heroines and crafting stories that resonate with emotional impact and strong sensuality. She's a Florida girl who has traveled the US, calling different states her home before crossing the pond to settle in the midlands of the UK, where she lives with her husband and a spoiled miniature dachshund. Find her on the web at www.katherinegarbera.com.

Books by Katherine Garbera

Harlequin Desire

One Night

One Night with His Ex
One Night, Two Secrets
One Night to Risk It All
Her One Night Proposal

Destination Wedding

The Wedding Dare
The One from the Wedding
Secrets of a Wedding Crasher

Visit her Author Profile page at Harlequin.com, or katherinegarbera.com, for more titles.

You can also find Katherine Garbera on Facebook, along with other Harlequin Desire authors, at Facebook.com/harlequindesireauthors!

To Charlotte and David Smith.
I wouldn't be who I am today without my parents.
They've taught me to never give up,
to laugh at myself, to be fiercely independent
and to be kind.
Love you more than I can say, Mom and Dad.

One

"Busted."

Melody Conner arched one eyebrow at the tall, dark, handsome man who had put a hand on her arm and leaned in to block her view of the rest of the Osborn-Williams wedding reception.

The deejay was doing his job keeping everyone entertained while they waited for the bride and groom to arrive.

"You caught me. But what is it you think I've done?" she asked. She'd found in life it was better to not give too much away.

"You're a wedding crasher," he said succinctly. "Are you from a tabloid?"

"No."

"Some other type of journalist?"

"Again, no. So now what?" she asked.

She'd crashed the reception hoping to meet this man. Dare Bisset. Eldest son of August Bisset and cousin to the bride. He was also the US senator chairing a committee that was working on a pharmaceutical bill to help make prescriptions affordable for everyone.

Which was why Melody was here at this exclusive Nantucket wedding. She'd just been hired as an assistant research manager by Johnny Rosemond, a prominent lawyer who normally worked for the pharmaceutical lobby and was currently working to block a bill coming before a subcommittee Senator Bisset was temporarily chairing. Johnny had tasked her to help lead a team of interns to research and prepare arguments for their case in front of the committee, and she'd thought it might be a good idea to meet the chair and find out what made Darien Bisset tick.

She'd been vacationing with her parents and twin brother at their house on Martha's Vineyard, and it had seemed like fate that the wedding was taking place so nearby. But the senator had spotted her the moment she'd entered the reception ballroom.

"Depends on what you're here for," he said. "Are you sure you're not with the press?"

"God, no."

He laughed. "That's a mark in your favor. Toby Osborn fan?"

"Do I look like I'm in my fifties?" she teased. Her mom was a huge Toby Osborn fan and had been the one to point out that the wedding was taking place so close by.

"Definitely not," he said.

"So…?"

"So?"

She wasn't sure if he already knew who would be presenting in front of him in DC on Tuesday or if he was just fishing. She'd come here for information and wasn't going to give up the game unless he figured it out himself.

"Stop playing with me. Why are you here?" he asked. "Adler and Nick have had enough surprises this weekend. They finally tied the knot and I'm not going to let anyone mess up this reception."

Of course, she'd seen the news about the groom, Nick Williams. The wedding had inadvertently revealed that he was August Bisset's illegitimate son. Which was almost ironic, because Nick had been raised by August's most bitter business rival. As if that wasn't enough, it turned out that Dare's brother Logan was Nick's secret twin, making the two enemies blood relations. It was enough to give anyone heartburn. She couldn't even imagine what it had done to Adler Osborn, society darling and star of the wedding event of the year.

"I was just curious. I'm staying at the hotel and my boyfriend bailed on this weekend, so I was in my room alone. I heard the music and figured I'd sneak in and have some fun," she lied. "I just was hoping to salvage a bit of my weekend in Nantucket."

He stared down at her, his gaze squarely meeting hers. She imagined he was trying to see if she was lying. But she'd been on debate team in college and had just finished getting her law degree and had been bluffing for longer than she could remember. She might only be twenty-six, but she felt that she came across older.

"I'm not sure that's the truth."

"What will it take to convince you?" she asked, fully prepared to walk away once she'd exhausted all of her options.

"Join me for a drink while we wait for the bride and groom?" he asked.

"I'm not entirely sure your motives are pure," she said.

"They aren't. I'm still not one hundred percent sure I believe you," he admitted with a grin that made a tingle go down her spine.

"So you're going to keep me close?" she asked.

"Indeed. 'Keep your friends close and your enemies closer' are words I live by," he said.

"Got a lot of enemies?" she asked.

"More than I'd like," he said, leading the way to the bar set up just off the dance floor. "Care to try the couple-themed cocktail?"

"What is it?" she asked, looking around his broad shoulders at the chalkboard on the bar that detailed the drinks available.

The Osborn-Williams cocktail was a moonshine and blackberry concoction. Sounded interesting, but moonshine went straight to her head, the way tequila affected some people. And since she was working, she didn't think flirting and getting naked was a good plan.

"I think I'll have champagne, please," she said.

"Good idea. Make it two," Dare said to the bartender.

Once they both had their drinks he hesitated. "I guess you don't have an assigned seat?"

"No. I was going to hang back and see if there were some empty spots."

"Come and sit at my family's table so I can keep an eye on you. I think there is room. I was supposed to bring a date but at the last minute she had to cancel."

"Sort of like me," she said, playing the part she'd assigned herself earlier.

"Yes. But Cami isn't my girlfriend. She's just my plus-one at events when I'm between—"

Melody laughed as he broke off his thought. She already knew that the thirty-eight-year-old senator was a playboy with a reputation for dating curvy, smart women. His average relationship lasted three months before he ended things. She'd been studying him, trying to create a profile for her team, so they'd know the best way to approach him.

But in person he was more dynamic than he'd been on the page. She'd known he had dark hair and light blue eyes, but in person his eyes were almost mercurial, changing between blue and gray depending on the light. His smile was wide and friendly and sent her heart racing.

There was more to Dare Bisset than she'd realized. And it was only the fact that she hated losing and wanted to impress her new boss that made her fight the attraction she felt toward him.

She wasn't about to do something hormonally driven and ruin her hard work. She was young and had her entire career in front of her and he was just a guy. A hot, sexy man she needed to figure out so she could best him when they were both back in DC.

She just hoped she could remember that.

He lifted his champagne flute toward her.

"To wedding crashers."

"To wedding bouncers," she said.

He threw his head back and laughed, which set off butterflies in her stomach.

"So, what's your name?" he asked. He liked her. She was fun and he didn't think she was here to cause trouble. But he also wasn't going to take any chances. Every single day they'd been on Nantucket had brought another nasty surprise, and he'd like for his maternal cousin to have at least one day that was scandal-free.

"Melody," she said.

"Very nice. I'm Dare."

"Just Dare?"

"You know who I am," he said. "What about you, no last name?"

"I guess you don't know who I am, do you? I figured it would add to the air of mystery."

"It does," he said. He liked the idea of keeping things light with her. "But it also just makes me a little suspicious of you. My parents and family really don't need any more trouble this weekend. So I'm going to ask you again why are you here?"

He was in the mood to let down his guard and have some fun tonight. And right now, the only threat he'd seen was Melody. Her name suited her. She was cute, smart and hot.

"There is no way for me to prove this. I was sitting in my room feeling sorry for myself and my bad judgment when it came to men. I heard the music and thought…it would be nice to just drink and dance and forget about life for a while."

He scrutinized her, watching her face for any giveaways or tells. He was used to his father, who was hard-as-nails but also tended to keep his true motives close to his chest. He wanted to believe her, she seemed sincere. But after the last few days he was disinclined to just trust.

He'd keep her close, so she didn't harm his family. And maybe he'd have a bit of fun with her. Maybe.

"I'll accept that. For now."

"Ha. Guess the rumors that you are a tough negotiator are true," she said.

"I have been getting a bit of a hard time thanks to the news coverage about my job," he said. He hadn't been the original senator asked to head the subcommittee overseeing an important pharmaceutical bill but when the ranking member had been implicated in an embezzling scheme, he'd stepped up. But that was the last thing he wanted to think about or discuss tonight. "What is it you do?"

"I work for a think tank in DC," she said. "Actually, it's my first job out of law school."

"Your first job? At a think tank? Impressive," he said. "For my first job, I interned with Bisset Industries."

"Is your father as hard to work for as I've heard?" she asked.

"Yes, Dare, is he?"

Dare glanced over his shoulder to see his parents standing there. His father was an older version of himself with hair that was now salt-and-pepper gray. His mother was gorgeous and aging gracefully, still looking a decade younger than her years. She had long blond hair that she was wearing in an elegant updo. And though she was only the bride's aunt, she'd functioned as the mother of the bride, having practically raised Adler when she wasn't with her father. His mom's only sister had died when Adler was a baby.

"Yes, he is," Dare said, turning to kiss his mom on the cheek. "But he definitely doesn't mind having that reputation. Mom and Dad, this is Melody. Melody, meet my parents, August and Juliette Bisset."

"Nice to meet you," Melody said, holding out her hand.

Both of his parents shook it and then his mom asked, "Are you a friend of Nick's or Adler's?"

He glanced at Melody, who seemed to be debating what she should say, then put his hand on the small of her back. "She's with me, Mom. She's from DC."

"Oh, I'm sorry I missed that detail. I'm so happy to meet you," his mom said, quickly moving the conversation forward and asking Melody how she'd enjoyed the ceremony.

He watched his mom step into her role as one of the hosts of the party. She'd always fallen back on her social skills and was a consummate professional when it came to projecting to the world that everything was okay. To everyone at the party his parents seemed like the affable couple they'd always been, as if the lies and secrets of thirty years ago that had resurfaced this weekend hadn't driven a wedge between them. He admired her calm in this moment.

"I see my brother just arrived, and I need to talk to him about some changes to the board," August said, dropping a kiss on Juliette's cheek before he met Dare's gaze. "Excuse me, son. Melody, it was nice to meet you and I look forward to getting to know you better."

His father left them and a few moments later his mother was called to handle a situation with the caterers. Dare turned back to Melody; her brown eyes followed the crowd as most of the guests started to arrive for the reception.

She had long blond hair that seemed like it might be highlighted; it suited her tan skin. Her face was heart-shaped and her mouth full. He knew better than to let his eyes linger on her lips, though he had a hard time not doing so. He was also so careful with his personal relationships but was influenced by the last few days seeing his brothers going after what they wanted—breaking out of the strict roles that they'd always followed. He was tempted by Melody and a part of him wanted to know what kissing that sassy mouth of hers would be like.

"Wow, your parents are…so good at socializing," she said after a pause.

"What do you mean by that?"

"I told you I read the news stories about everything going on with your family. If my parents were in their shoes my mom would be giving my dad the cold shoulder and if he dared touch her or kiss her cheek, she'd probably elbow him in the gut."

Dare couldn't help laughing at that. "I see where you get that sassiness from."

"You're right, I am just like her. I hate that kind of subterfuge."

"Is there a kind you do like?" he asked.

"Well, sometimes you have to behave a certain way to get results. You probably know more about that than most," she said. "Like my mom won't tolerate my brother and me trying to one-up each other, so we have to be subtle about it."

"Do you compete a lot?" he asked. What she was saying about her brother reminded him of his relationship with his siblings.

"All the time," she said. "I think if our family had

a motto it would be 'Winner takes all and second place is first loser.'"

"That's harsh," he said.

"It's realistic. Better to set the expectation at the start of any relationship, my dad always says. I like to win and I won't apologize for it."

Apparently August was a lot like her father, which was why Dare had chosen politics for his career instead of following his father into the family business. Arguably politics was the easier of the two paths as he didn't have to follow August's rules and live in his shadow. Dare had never been one to do that.

"Agreed," he said. The deejay directed everyone to find their tables and Dare wasn't surprised to see Melody's name on the card at the spot next to his. His mom was thorough that way. And it gave legitimacy to her presence by his side, which he knew shouldn't matter but somehow did.

"So how did you meet my brother?"

"Which Bisset are you?"

The man laughed and shook his head. "Zac, America's Cup captain and team leader. Date to Iris Collins, the maid of honor."

He was an outdoorsy-looking, handsome guy, but not as good-looking as Dare, she thought.

"To answer your question, I met your brother at this hotel," she said, glancing to her left at Dare and winking at him. "The moment he spotted me he couldn't resist me."

"That sounds sus to me," he said, clearly trying to needle Dare.

She had to admit there was an element of fun in being with Dare at this table with his family that she hadn't had in a long time. She was working hard to rise to the top in a very competitive field and a part of her warned against letting down her guard. But as the evening had worn on, it didn't seem that dangerous.

"I didn't have to bribe her, Zac, if that's what you were trying to find out," Dare said. "Old Zac here was paid to be—"

"We have just resolved that," Zac cut him off. "I don't think Iris would like to hear it brought up again and I'll do whatever it takes to keep her happy."

She'd read all of the gossip about Zac and Iris Collins. Iris was a high profile influencer with her own lifestyle television show. Apparently her boyfriend had dumped her just days before Adler's wedding and Iris had hired Zac to be her boyfriend. Apparently they'd fallen for each other.

Dare put his hand up. "Down, boy. I didn't mean anything by it. Just saying that there isn't anything fishy between me and Melody."

"Tell me more about what you do, Zac?" she asked, changing the subject because she had the feeling the brothers weren't willing to just let it go.

"As I said, I captain an America's Cup team. I had been working for another team. In fact, while I'm here in New England I'm raising capital for my own team."

"That's interesting," she said.

"Which means boring, right?" he asked.

"Which means I don't know much about it," she admitted. "I dated a guy who rowed crew in college."

"Yeah? Where'd you go? I rowed crew, too," Zac said.

"Georgetown," she said.

"They have a good team," Zac said. He looked like he was going to ask her more about rowing, but a gorgeous blonde bridesmaid came over and put her hand on the center of his back and leaned down to whisper in his ear and he turned away.

"Iris?" she asked Dare.

"Yes. She's way too good for my brother," Dare said loudly after Iris went back to the head table.

Zac shot him the bird and then got up. "I have to go dance with Iris."

Zac left them and Melody noticed that many of the other people at their table were getting up. Including Juliette, who turned to Zac.

"That means you two as well," she said. "After the first dance, Adler is doing a family dance."

"We'll be there," Dare said.

Melody swallowed a bit at the thought of being included in this. She had a feeling that he wasn't going to be able to just forgive this kind of deception. For a minute she wondered if she should excuse herself and walk out of the ballroom and away from Dare.

"I did have a sort of John Travolta–style *Satur-*

day Night Fever routine prepared but now that you're here… I guess I won't be dancing alone."

She knew she couldn't leave. There was something in his tone that made him…well, more human. Not just someone to further her career.

Juliette went toward the dance floor as Toby Osborn, along with his drummer and bass guitarist, took over from the deejay. Toby had his acoustic guitar and Melody realized he was going to perform live. Her mom would love to hear this.

"Do you think I could video this and send it to my mom? Or is that tacky?" she asked Dare as he stood and pulled out her chair.

"You can video it for your mom. Come on, let's get closer. I think he's going to perform a song he wrote especially for Adler."

He did. It was a heartrending ballad that didn't leave a dry eye in the house. Even Dare blinked a few times. Nick and Adler danced together as Toby sang about watching his little girl grow up and the pride he felt at the woman she'd become. It was classic Toby Osborn but so personal it almost made Melody wish she hadn't recorded it. But not enough for her to delete the video.

Everyone burst into applause when he was done. He came over to Adler and kissed her. It was such a sweet moment, making Melody cringe at the thought that she was here under false pretenses. She had a few second thoughts about trying to get information from Dare.

"Now it's time for the family dance," the deejay said from the stage. "We Are Family" by Sister Sledge started up.

"Do you want to send that before we dance?" Dare asked, pointing to her phone.

"No way. I want to see your moves," she said, taking his hand and leading him out on the dance floor close to Zac and Iris.

Zac smiled at her and they all danced in a circle soon joined by his other brothers and the Williams siblings. It was interesting to her to see them all intermingling, because she knew there was a fierce rivalry between the Williams and Bisset families.

She did note that August and Juliette were in the circle with the bride and groom and Nick's parents. The two men looked a bit awkward, like they were competing to see who had the smoother moves.

"Oh, for f's sake," Dare said. "Dad is trying to outdance Tad."

"And he's winning," said a stunning woman dancing with the groom's family. "I'm Olivia Williams, by the way. Nick's sister. Our dad only has dad dance moves."

"I'm not seeing anything different from ours," Zac said. "We should go rescue them."

"Agreed," said Iris.

The bride's and groom's siblings advanced toward their parents, and Melody watched the careful way that they made sure to make it look like they were all one big happy comingled group. But it was clear that the dads weren't the only ones trying to outdance each other. The kids were, too, which made her feel a bit better about her reasons for being with Dare.

He came from a very competitive family that wasn't going to let their rivals win even at something as trivial as a family dance. And as the evening wore on and she partied with Dare, she realized that he was the leader of the pack.

She couldn't help it: she was attracted to him. As she drank more champagne, all the reasons for not getting too close while she gathered intel fell away in her mind. Soon it seemed logical that hooking up would be the perfect end to this evening.

Two

"Want to get some fresh air?" Dare asked Melody after the bride and groom left. The party had been fun and she'd been a good companion, but he was feeling edgy and like he needed a cigarette, even though he'd quit over ten years ago. The fact that Melody had made him laugh didn't have to mean anything. Hell, he was at least ten years older than her and even though for the first time in days he felt like he could breathe, this couldn't be more than tonight.

So taking a break should be more like *see ya*. He knew that, but then she looked up at him with those wide eyes and he felt an electric pulse of desire. They'd been touching and dancing. She'd been vague in her answers at times and then at others sincere, taking a video to send to her mom. He could relate to that.

"Love to. I'm ready for a break from dancing," she said.

He put his hand on the small of her back and led her away from the dance floor and the noise out onto the terrace that overlooked the gardens behind the hotel. The decor from the reception extended to out here. He found them a bench near a fountain to sit down.

"So, party crasher, has this evening been everything you had hoped?" he asked her wryly. This attraction to her could be dangerous. He liked to think of himself as smart enough to learn from the mistakes he'd seen his father make and the last few days had pulled the lid off a can of worms he had no intention of repeating in his life. Attraction was dangerous. As a Bisset and as a senator, he thought he was more aware of this than many others. Still, he'd be lying if he said he didn't want her more than he should.

Earlier on the dance floor she'd pulled an elastic from her purse and put her hair up in a ponytail. A few tendrils curled around the sides of her face and gave her a softer look than she'd had when he'd first approached her. Right now she came across as too young to be up to something. But age was no guarantee of innocence. In fact he knew he wouldn't have approached Melody if she'd first had this innocent look. But the other way she'd seemed more professional and calculating, like she had an agenda she was trying to pursue.

She'd said she was on a research team. That could mean anything.

Perhaps he'd gotten cynical, used to life in DC. And of course this weekend, being a Bisset had put them all in the spotlight, so he'd assumed an uninvited guest like her had a nefarious motive.

"I have definitely forgotten about old what's-his-name who ghosted me," she said with a quick smile.

"Who would ghost you?" he asked, trying to make sure there weren't holes in her story that he'd missed. "Guy must be an idiot."

She smiled and shook her head. "Thanks. He's not. He just thought it was too soon for a weekend away together. I guess he was right."

"A weekend away. Is that a serious step for you?" Dare asked. Because it wouldn't be for him. Growing up as August Bisset's son, Dare had realized that he and his father didn't have a lot in common, but the few traits they did share—well, those didn't bode well for long-term relationships. His six-month marriage in his twenties had proven that. He didn't want to test his belief that he very different from his father on the inside. The last thing he wanted in his life was to end up treating a woman the way his father had treated his mother.

"Not really. But you know, going away for the weekend can just be fun," she said, looking out in the distance.

He sensed there was more she wasn't telling him. Maybe the guy who'd stood her up meant more to her than she wanted to let on. Love was weird like that. Dare had never trusted the emotion when it came to intimate relationships. How could one person fall deeply in love while their partner felt only light affection? It wasn't something he'd ever really taken the time to explore.

"I get it. I'm the same way. Sometimes you want something casual at the beach," he said lightly.

"Exactly. What about your plus one?"

"Cami? She just fills in at family events when I need a date. I'm pretty much a workaholic. Growing up watching my mom try to manage the family while my dad was always working gave me an inside view of how hard that can be on a partner," Dare said. "Any woman I seriously care about…well, I wouldn't want to put her in that position."

"That's really intuitive. Most guys are just looking to get laid," she said.

"Well, that, too," he said. This conversation was entering dangerous territory. They were essentially strangers. He had felt that spark between them when they danced and he knew it wasn't one-sided. She'd looked at him a few times like she wanted more. But fun? He was old enough to know better. But damn if after the weekend he'd had he just wanted to let go and have fun. Have something that didn't end up turning into a scandal. He was beginning to realize that if anyone could test his self-control, it was this woman.

"So…?" she asked.

He didn't know how to respond and she turned and leaned into him. She put her hand in the center of his chest and her eyes dilated, her breath going out on a long sigh. Then she went up on tiptoe and ran her finger over his lips. "There is something about you…."

"Maybe it's just that I know your secret."

Her eyes widened and she chewed her lower lips between her teeth. This close to him she was temptation incarnate and it was all he could do to keep himself from lowering his head to kiss her. He was getting hard, and the reasons why he shouldn't take what he wanted were getting less and less important to him.

"Maybe. Are you suddenly suspicious of me again?"

"Not suspicious of you. Just afraid to follow my instincts where you are concerned." But he wasn't. His instincts said kiss her, stop talking to her. His gut said to follow his Bisset DNA and take what he wanted, damned the consequences. And there might be some. She was complicated. She might not be over the guy who'd stood her up. He needed to be sensible.

But there were times when being sensible sucked. And this was one of them. He wanted to be like his father or Logan and just reach out and take what he wanted. Why shouldn't he?

"Oh?"

He scooted closer to her on the bench and putting his arm on the back of it so that he could touch her bare shoulder with his hand.

She shivered delicately under his touch and turned her head until their eyes met. It was hard to read her expression and guess at her emotions, but her body was sending clear signals. Her skin was flushed, her pupils dilated, and her lips parted. She leaned in closer and he inhaled the sweet scent of her perfume. Something summery with floral undertones. She put her hand on his thigh and a tingle went straight through him. He shifted his legs a little as he hardened and licked his lips.

"I want you," he admitted. "I don't know what you have in mind for the rest of the evening and I don't want to pressure you in any way."

"Because you're a senator and don't want a scandal later?" she asked.

"Because I'm a man who respects women," he said. Scandal was second nature to him but treating a woman like she owed him something wasn't in his programming.

"I like you, Dare. More than I should," she said.

"Is that good or bad?"

"I haven't decided yet," she said.

He held his breath for a moment. He held her gaze, moving his hand up her shoulder to the back of her neck. It was faintly sweaty from the dancing they'd done earlier. He leaned in, watching her eyes start to close, and then brushed his lips over hers and kissed her long and deep.

She tasted good. Better than good. She set off a chain reaction inside him that he hadn't felt in a long time. Her hand dug into his thigh and she shifted closer, her other arm coming around his shoulder to draw him to her.

When he lifted his head a few moments later, she winked at him and said, "Guess there is definitely a spark."

Dare kissed like a man who knew what he wanted and wasn't in a hurry to get it. He made her feel like she had all the time in the world. His touch on her neck was subtle yet firm and he held her loosely, not pawing at her body the way some of the men she'd dated had. There was a refinement to him that turned her on.

Her conscience niggled at the thought of sleeping with him when she was going to go home and write down all her impressions in a dossier so her boss could figure out the best way to leverage him and get the results he wanted. This had bad idea written all over it. She was smarter than this. She had to be.

But Senator Darien Bisset had surprised her. He had been careful to keep her close so she couldn't hurt anyone else in his family. He'd treated her fairly and with respect.

She wished she'd never come out here with him. He kept staring at her and she did wonder if she was making a wise decision. But she knew that come Tuesday, the employee with the most complete picture of Dare Bisset was going to be the one to the lead the team to a big win. And Melody was ready to prove herself. She had to. She wasn't going to settle for being second.

And he'd just said this was fun, nothing more. They were having a good night, had been dancing and grinding against each other until she'd been turned on and so had he. This kiss…it was the natural next step. Was she really going to do this? If she did…it was an ethical breech. Or was it? She hadn't asked him anything about the pharmaceutical bill he was working on. All she'd done was flirt with him, watch him with his family and now kiss him.

"No pressure here. Destination weddings always feel like they aren't real life," he said. "But we both know that they are."

"You're right. I wasn't expecting to be with you."

"I wasn't either," he admitted. "And I can't take you back to my place. I'm staying at my grandmother's house…"

"I have a hotel room, remember?" she said. "Not sure that meeting your grandmother is something that either of us wants tonight."

"Agreed. I'll need to stop by the gift shop," he said.

"Why?" she asked. "You can just wear those clothes tomorrow."

"I was thinking about protection. If you're sure about this," he said.

"Oh, duh. I'm on the pill," she said. No way was she going to let her life get derailed by a baby. Not now. She had a plan and it included kids when she was in her thirties after she'd gotten her career on track and was kicking ass as a world-class boss babe.

"I'll still stop," he said.

"You're very cautious," she said.

"Yeah, well, my dad just found out about a kid he fathered thirty years ago," Dare said.

He had to be looking for a way to blow off some steam. She could use that too. They were just Dare and Melody. She was done with her research, she told herself. From the moment they'd come onto the balcony he was just a man she wanted.

"Good point. But just so you know, if I did wind up pregnant, you'd be my first call," she said.

"But why take unnecessary chances? I want this night to be the kind of perfect memory that neither of us regrets," he said.

"Me, too," she admitted. She felt slightly bad about the fact that she'd come to the reception to get information on him. He seemed like a decent man. The kind of man she'd really like to be on a date with. But they would never have met if she hadn't taken the initiative and come here tonight.

He put his hand on the small of her back, directing her into the reception hall. She liked the way he did that. A part of her knew it was an old-fashioned gesture and normally she'd be annoyed, but he did it in such a way that it felt almost like he was trying to protect her from everyone else. It made her feel— *stop it.* She felt lust.

That was all she was going to allow herself to feel. It had been way too long since she'd hooked up.

He waved goodbye to his brothers and sister and then they left the ballroom. The hallway was oddly quiet after the noise of the party and as they entered the lobby, he hesitated.

"I'm in room two-twenty," she said.

"I'll meet you up there."

She walked away from him toward the bank of elevators. When she got to her room, she checked her phone and saw her mom had responded with the heart eyes emoji to the video that Melody had sent earlier of Toby Osborn singing.

Her mom had once said if she could communicate in real life with just emojis she'd be a happy woman. Of course, that was before she'd realized that the poo emoji wasn't chocolate ice cream. Melody smiled thinking about her mom. She didn't know the real reason Melody was at the reception; Melody had simply told her that it was a work thing.

She knew her parents wouldn't approve of her methods. But they weren't really on her mind. It was only Dare. Dare with his thick black hair, strong jaw and body that had felt so hard and strong when she'd brushed against him.

She slipped off her shoes and went into the bathroom to take down her ponytail and brush her teeth. She did a quick check of the room and made sure that there wasn't anything out that would give her away to Dare. Then she heard his knock.

She walked over to check the peephole before opening the door. He was carrying a gift store bag.

"Get what you needed?"

"I did," he said, hesitating on the threshold as if he didn't want to assume that she was still hot for him. "Still want me here?"

"Yes," she said. More than he could know. She had been trying to talk herself out of this but one look at him and her pulse raced. This wasn't logical. It was something she wanted. "Did you think I'd change my mind?"

"It could happen," he said carefully.

"It didn't."

And he was too much of a gentleman to push his advantage. She had another sting of her conscience. Was this the wrong thing to do?

But before she could decide, he was inside the room, closing the door behind him and pulling her into his arms. His kiss was fierce this time, full of passion, and she met him on the same level of intensity.

Her tongue tangled with his as she put her arms around his shoulders and went up on tiptoe to deepen the kiss. He gave her everything he had, and she took it all. He lifted her off her feet and turned so that he was leaning against the wall, and she pressed herself along the front of his body.

* * *

Her room was neat and tidy, which fit the image
of the woman he'd first met. All perfectly polished,
with some sort of agenda. But it didn't fit her now.
She had all but lost control, with her hands in his
hair and her body flush against his.

He found the zipper on the side of her dress and
slowly drew it down until he could push his hand underneath the fabric. Her skin was cool to the touch.
He ran his finger down the length of her spine and
then cupped her butt, pulling her more firmly against
him. She tore her mouth from his, and resting her
forehead against his, she opened her eyes. They were
so close he thought they should be able to see right
into each other's souls.

But this wasn't soul sex. This was a hot, one-night
stand. Something to blow off the steam that had been
building since he'd arrived on Nantucket. That was
all it could be. They had nothing in common.

She shifted away from him, taking his free hand
and pulling him farther into the room toward the
bed. He followed her.

She had let her hair down and when she turned
it flowed around her shoulders. She reached for the
hem of her dress and pulled it up and over her head,
tossing it toward the chair in the corner.

He caught his breath at the sight of her in just a
strapless bra and a pair of tiny bikini panties. She
had full breasts and a small waist; her stomach had

a tiny little bump and her legs were curvy. She stood there staring at him, with one hand on her hip.

"Um, one of us is way ahead of the other one," she said.

"Sorry, I was enjoying the view," he said.

"I'd like to as well. Do you need some help?"

"Are you offering?"

"I am."

"Then, yes," he said. "I could definitely use some help."

He toed off his shoes and kicked them behind him, then took off his dress socks. She was at his side, tugging at his tie and loosening it as he shrugged out of his jacket. He tossed it toward the table by the chair and it landed on it. She pulled his tie back and forth in the collar of his shirt, using it to draw him toward her, and he realized that he was completely in her web.

That he wanted nothing more than to do whatever this woman wanted from him. The more turned on she got, the more he did. Her pleasure was feeding his. She leaned up and sucked his bottom lip between her teeth as she slowly undid the buttons of his shirt. He felt the brush of her knuckles as her hands made their way down his body.

She broke the kiss and stepped back, pushing his dress shirt down his shoulders. He wore a white T-shirt underneath, and she shook her head. "You have on too many clothes, Dare. Get naked."

Her words shot through him, making him hard

and forcing him to step away from her. He undid the buttons at his wrists and took off his dress shirt, then whipped the T-shirt over his head and tossed it aside before he turned back to face her.

"Better?"

"You're getting there," she said.

She moved closer and touched his chest. He had a fair amount of hair on his body, and had dated a few women in the past who didn't like it. But Melody didn't seem to mind. She ran her hands over his torso, slowly working her way to down to his stomach.

She undid his belt and then unfastened his pants and lowered the zipper. She pushed her hand into the opening of his trousers, stroking him through his briefs and he had to put his hand over hers to stop her for a moment. He was close to the edge and it was too soon.

He put his other arm around her waist and drew her closer to him, feeling the brush of her stomach against his as she undid the clasp of her strapless bra with one hand. She leaned back and tossed it away and then tightened her embrace, her breasts cushioned against him. He walked backward to the bed with her in his arms, then turned and gently pushed her down onto it. He took a condom out of the box he'd bought at the gift shop and put it on the nightstand while he finished taking off his clothes.

She arched her hips and pushed her underwear off, then lay there on the bed before him, totally naked. Her blond hair was spread out around her head, and she couldn't look more inviting. He took the condom and put it on before coming onto the bed. He caressed her breasts as she parted her legs.

He held himself braced on his arms and looked down into her eyes. She caught his hard-on in her hand and drew him forward. He reached between her legs to see if she as ready for him. She was.

He captured her mouth in a kiss and drove himself inside her. She arched her back to take him deeper, wrapping her legs around his hips. She met him thrust for thrust, driving him higher and higher, and he knew he was going to come quicker than he had in a long time.

He reached between their bodies and found her clit, touching and rubbing it until he felt her arching against him with more urgency. Then her body tightened around him and she called his name out loud. He held her hips and drove himself into her, thrusting, driving into her with more strength until he felt like he was going to explode. He felt her tightening around him, clenching against his cock. She cried out his name and then he let himself go. Driving into her again and again until he came long and hard. He continued to thrust until he was spent, then he shifted to his side, drawing her into his arms. Holding her as if she was his for more than just this one night, until he realized what he was doing.

He loosened his hold and looked down at her. She stared up at him with a satisfied smile on her face. "Well, that was nice."

Three

Melody woke with a start, feeling a large warm man cuddled behind her on the bed. She took a moment to remember where she was and whom she was with. The hotel room was dimly lit and the clock on the dresser read 2:13 a.m. It was dark and a sliver of moonlight came in through the part in the curtains. She'd been in a hurry to get things ready for him and hadn't closed them all the way.

Dare.

Darien Bisset.

She'd crashed a wedding to get intel on him for her job. And she was still determined to get it, no matter how complicated things were now. She felt a tinge of guilt. Okay, more than a twinge. But she was actually going to have to do some snooping through his personal stuff. He hadn't really given much away. She'd planned to use the things she'd learned about him over the evening to help write her profile. So far, she knew he was a very loyal person. He didn't back down when it came to supporting the people in his inner circle.

He was also very competitive and from what she could tell not someone she wanted to cross.

But was that enough to help her boss find an edge over him? She doubted it. And as much as she'd enjoyed the sex with Dare, she wanted to take home more than that.

He was snoring, so she was pretty sure he was sound asleep. She got out of bed quietly. He rolled over and stopped snoring, and she froze, waiting to see what he'd do next. She heard his breathing start to deepen again.

She picked up his clothes off the floor to straighten them and his wallet and phone fell out.

Was that a sign? She couldn't riffle through his wallet without it being cringey, even for her. But she glanced at his phone as she moved to set it down and the lock screen had three notifications on it. She was curious about them. She shouldn't look at them. But then again, they were right there on the phone. Maybe if they popped up again, she'd just have a peek. She turned the phone again and saw the first was from his mom saying good-night.

That was innocuous. Nothing wrong with Melody seeing that one.

That was something her mom did every night and she thought it was sweet that his mom did it, too. It sort of made Melody feel like a Peeping Thomasina doing this. But she tilted her hand again to make the notifications reappear, and this time saw there was one from Hank Cooper. He was on the house sub-committee also working on a pharmaceutical bill similar to the one that Dare was chairing in the Senate. His message was truncated, and she could only read the first part.

Turnball having second thoughts. Wants to meet...

Turnball?

Bill Turnball? It had to be him. He was one of the biggest lobbyists for the pharmaceutical industry on Capitol Hill. He had been one of the most outspo-ken opponents of the committee being formed. He wanted no part of the reform that the public had been demanding. As a matter of fact, he'd been one of the first people her team had talked to. Was he working both sides of this issue? Trying to sweet-talk the Sen-ate and house committees while feeding her boss a story? She needed to look into that.

There was one more notification, but she was wor-ried she was taking too long putting Dare's phone down. She flicked her wrist and skimmed the third one and saw it was just that he'd been tagged in a photo on social media.

She blanched. If they were photographed together, she was busted and not just by Dare. Her boss wouldn't like it at all. He'd said to be discreet if she tried to get close to Bisset and his team.

This wasn't good, she thought.

Quickly, she put his phone down on the pile of his clothes, reached for her phone where she'd left it on the dresser and took it into the bathroom. She logged on to Instagram and skimmed for pictures of Dare, and luckily she wasn't really visible in any of them. She saw the back of her head when they were dancing and one where Dare was holding her during a slow dance, but her face wasn't visible.

Damn.

She hadn't even considered social media. She'd just felt that spark of awareness from the moment he'd come up to her at the reception and gone for it. How many times had her impulsiveness gotten her into trouble? Too many to count. She needed to stop following her gut and start using her head.

She took a deep breath and typed up the notes that she had regarding what she'd read on his phone and then her impressions of him that evening. Then she quietly went back to bed, crawling in next to Dare. He reached for her and pulled her into his arms.

"You okay?"

"Yes. Needed a drink of water," she lied. He mumbled and just pulled her closer to him. She tried to close her eyes and go back to sleep but she couldn't.

She liked working to get ahead and she was never afraid of taking risks. But this felt wrong to her as it was almost certainly illegal. She wanted to win but not by cheating, and wasn't this a big cheat?

A part of her said it was research. All great generals knew their enemy before they went into battle with them, which was all she was doing.

But why then did she feel that lump in the pit of her stomach? She tried to close her eyes and picture her future life. That always calmed her down and helped her to sleep but even when she dozed off her dreams were troubled, and she didn't sleep well.

She finally fell asleep with no more clarity over what she had done and if she was actually going to use the information she found.

She woke a few hours later to the smell of coffee. Dare sat on the edge of the bed dressed in a branded Nantucket T-shirt and a pair of golf shorts that he must have purchased last night.

"Good morning, Melody."

Dare had woken early as was his habit. No matter how late he stayed up he always was wide-awake at five.

For a while, he'd watched Melody sleeping next to him and had a few of those thoughts that sometimes floated through his mind. The settling-down ones. What would his life be like if he had someone to come to home to? He knew that that woman wasn't Melody. She'd pretty much stated that the night before.

And he'd always been a little too much like his

dad for Dare to feel comfortable tying himself to one woman. He had a genuine love and appreciation for most women and liked the fact that he'd always been honest with the women he'd been involved with. He had always feared that if he made a commitment to one woman, he'd have a hard time sticking to it.

His father had certainly had a hard time being faithful to his mother. It hadn't really hurt August, just his family. But Dare knew that he wasn't as brazen as his father when it came to taking what he wanted at the cost of those who cared for him.

Dare had taken a shower and dressed in the clothing he'd picked up in the gift shop when he'd gotten the condoms last night. Melody had slept soundly through all of it, including his ordering breakfast and coffee for them both. He had some work he needed to do but he'd never been the kind of man to leave while a woman was sleeping. That had always seemed rude to him. He knew his brother Logan had done it a time or two because according to him it ensured that there were no awkward conversations.

"Morning. Is that coffee for me?"

"It is," Dare said, handing her the mug. "Not sure how you take it."

"Black is great," she said, taking the cup from him and then looking at it. "Or with cream."

He smiled. "And two sugars."

"And two sugars," she said. She took a sip, closed her eyes and sighed. "That's really good. I haven't had sugar in my coffee since I left for college. I forgot how good it tastes."

"I like to start the day on a sweet note," he said. He had an addiction for sweet coffee and doughnuts in the morning, which he only indulged when he was on vacation. At home he kept himself on a strict diet. "I ordered a bit of everything for breakfast if you're hungry."

"I am," she said. "I'll go and wash up and then we can eat."

She hopped out of bed and he had glimpse of her naked body as she took her coffee to the bathroom. He'd been tempted to make love to her again but didn't want to feed his addiction for her. There was no future with her and the sooner he got out of her hotel room and back to his real life the better it would be for him.

He moved their clothes off the table, having noticed that sometime in the night she'd folded all the clothing, including his, and set it there. He set up their breakfast and replied to the texts from his grandmother asking if she'd see him again before he left Nantucket. He told her he'd definitely stop by. There were also two from his assistant and then one from Mari asking to fly back with him on his jet to New York.

It was a busy morning and he had wanted to give Melody his sole attention before his world started pulling him back. But he knew it was too late. He was already thinking of the things he had to do and counting the minutes until he left.

She joined him a few moments later. Her hair had been tamed into a thick braid and she had on a robe embroidered with the hotel logo. She sat across from him and lifted the cloche from the plate in front of her.

"You weren't kidding when you said you got everything."

"I didn't know what you liked." He'd realized that as he was sitting here waiting for her to wake up. She was essentially a stranger and he knew that was for the best, but a part of him wished it could be different. But another part of him knew it couldn't be. She had no place in his real world, he hadn't been joking when he'd said he was a workaholic, and he liked his job. That made relationships difficult, to say the least, and no one knew that better than him. Also she was young. She should find someone who wasn't as jaded as he was.

"Eggs and bacon, but I normally have a green smoothie," she said. "It's healthy and honestly the only way I get my greens in. For some reason when I drink a smoothie, it doesn't seem as bad as a plate of broccoli does."

She was rambling talking about the food and he realized she might be nervous.

"You okay?"

"Yeah. Just…normally guys don't stick around and I'm really not sure what to do."

"I wasn't sure. It feels weird to just leave," he said. "Should I go now?"

"No. I sort of like having you here."

"What are you going to be doing for the rest of the day? When are you leaving?"

"I'm probably going to do some shopping and then I'm booked on the last ferry. How about you?"

"I'm leaving once we're done with breakfast and I say goodbye to my grandmother. I have a ton of work waiting for me back home. This week was supposed to be a vacation but it wasn't as relaxing as I'd hoped."

"Some weekends are like that," she said.

"Most of the time I can relax. But usually I'm not surrounded by my family and their business rivals."

She laughed and nodded. "That does tend to make a vacation a little stressful."

The conversation stalled because there wasn't any future to a one-night stand.

They finished breakfast.

"So you work in DC?"

"I do," she said.

"Should we exchange numbers?" he asked.

"Should we? Do you feel like you have to?" she asked, chewing her bottom lip between her teeth. "Like you said last night, this was a moment out of time. You don't have to do anything."

He nodded. "Okay, well then… I guess I should say goodbye and let you get back to your life."

He stood up, gathering his suit, which he'd carefully placed in the laundry bag from the hotel. Then after one more long look between them, he turned and walked away. He knew he'd never see her again, but this night had been fun and a memory that he would treasure for a long time to come.

"Of course, I'm jealous that you actually got to go to the reception. Did you get close to Toby Osborn at all?" her mom asked as she sat on Melody's bed watching her pack up her things to go to DC in the morning.

"No, I didn't. He was sort of being a dad to the bride and I figured the last thing he wanted to do was pose for a selfie with me," Melody said.

"That's so cool. This new job of yours has some nice perks," her mom said. "I wish you could stay at the beach longer but maybe you can come back in August before we go home."

"Maybe," Melody said, knowing she wasn't going to come. She liked being at the beach but truthfully if she took another vacation in August, she was going to leave the door open for a coworker, maybe even one of the interns on her team, to pass her by and that wasn't happening. "My job is going to be pretty busy. We have a lot to prepare to get ready for the presentation before Congress. I don't know if I'll get back, but maybe you and Dad can come visit me in Washington."

"We definitely will," her mom said. "I'll go check the dryer and see if your clothes are done."

Her mom left and Melody dropped the smile she'd been forcing since…well, since Dare had left her hotel room before noon.

She didn't know what was wrong with her. Politics wasn't like a quilting bee or something homey where everyone came together. It was strategy and tactics and she'd made a play. There wasn't anything wrong with that. She'd always played to win.

For the first time she wondered if she should be playing for something else, but honestly, she had no idea what. She couldn't play and not try to win. That wasn't something that was in her. She couldn't figure it out. To be fair this was the first time she'd slept with the enemy.

Gah.

Now she sounded like she was in a cheesy made-for-TV movie.

Her phone pinged and she glanced down to see it was a message from Aubrey.

She was another of the researchers working for Johnny Rosemond's team and they'd really clicked when they'd met last month.

Hey girl! How's Martha's Vineyard? Did you find anything on DB? I have a few things but he's pretty straitlaced. Not much dirt.

Melody was cagey in her response. Hey! MV is okay too many tourists. ;) I did find a few things. I'm already working on the profile.

What???? Spill.

Girl, do your own digging. :)

Fair enough. Coffee at 9 tomorrow?

Wouldn't miss it.

She put her phone back on the bed and finished packing. She was glad that she and Aubrey were having coffee as they were both competing for the top spot at work, but she needed to talk to someone about Dare and she couldn't with Aubrey. Her brother had gone clamming with their dad this morning before she'd gotten back to Martha's Vineyard. Hopefully Ben would be back before she had to leave to catch her late flight back to DC.

He was always a good sounding board and he'd help her get her mind back in the game.

But Ben didn't make it back before her flight. He'd run into some friends and gone sailing with them instead, so she was stuck with her own thoughts.

Which didn't really help; she kept remembering how Dare had felt in her arms. She needed to clear her head. Travel sort of helped with that; as she went through the airports then got a cab back to her apartment in Crystal City, she didn't think of him at all. When she let herself in and set down her bags, she looked around at the place she was calling home. It was small but in a good neighborhood. She was saving to buy her own place, paying her dues. And she knew that if she kept her eye on the prize, she'd get to her goal faster.

Yeah, that made a lot more sense. She'd been feeling sentimental today because she'd met Dare at a wedding and those kinds of events always stirred up the schmaltzy feelings that she preferred to ignore.

She sat at her desk, fired up her laptop and started her research on Turnball. She found that he'd recently been fired by People's RX, the group he'd been working for, which made him a loose cannon.

She spent all night working on her notes and when it was time to go to bed, she congratulated herself on not having done an internet search on Dare. In fact, even as she'd done research for the presentation before his committee, she had almost entirely avoided thinking about him as a man. Not a big deal since she was totally over her one-night stand. He had been one night of fun and that was all she'd needed.

But as she rolled over to go to sleep, she realized that she was reaching for him. That she remembered what it had been like to sleep in his arms.

Damn.

She didn't miss him.

Really, she told herself firmly, and used some deep breathing techniques to fall asleep, but she woke from a hot dream where he'd been making love to her in his office on Capitol Hill and finally got out of bed to take a shower and work some more.

She had to get him out of her head. And the only way to do that was to keep working, which wasn't helping since she was writing a report about him. She wasn't sure how to separate her guilty emotions from the report she wrote. Finally she just admitted she wasn't going to be able to compartmentalize Dare. She had her report finished before six, then went for a run, trying to get some distance from the memories of being in Dare's arms. But she couldn't, she realized.

When she went to join Aubrey for coffee, her co-worker was a bit too chatty considering that Melody hadn't slept well the night before. It was all she could do not to tell the other woman to stop talking so much. She realized she was on edge. Was it simply nerves, hoping her research would be the most in-depth and net her the job as head of the team? Or was it guilt? And maybe a little lust because one night with Dare hadn't been enough. Even though she knew it was all she'd ever have.

"I'm kind of nervous about presenting our ideas at the research meeting this morning."

"Why?" Melody asked as they left the coffee shop to head to their offices. "You're one of the top researchers in our group."

"Thanks, but you were so vague in your text. Makes me think you have the scoop," Aubrey said.

"I've got some good stuff," Melody admitted. "I think it will help us when we go in to get the ball rolling."

"I knew it. I heard you were someone to watch."

"Good," Melody said. "You definitely should. I heard the same about you."

"We should make a good team," Aubrey said.

Melody smiled but didn't comment. She didn't have any desire to share the glory with someone else. She'd live or die on her own sword. Even if that sword was Darien Bisset.

Four

It was always hard for Dare to say goodbye to his grandmother. He was particularly close to her because when he was little his parents were having a rough time and she'd ended up watching him. He'd also been close to Adler's mom, his aunt Musette, but she'd died when Dare was eight.

Now, sitting next to Gran on the bench she used to sit on with his grandfather and watching the ocean in the distance soothed Dare as nothing else ever did. "I bet you never thought going back to Washington would be a respite," she said, as the warm summer breeze blew around them.

The rest of the family was off somewhere on the island or lounging in the house. He'd found Gran sitting out here as soon as he'd gotten back from breakfast with Melody.

"Never. But it wasn't all bad, was it?" he asked.

"I didn't think so but then I'm too old for scandals to bother me," she said.

"Gran, you're not that old," he said, putting his arm around her shoulders and hugging her.

"I felt it a few days last week. But this morning with Adler and Nick married and seeming happy… I do feel younger," she admitted. "What about you? I saw you dancing with a pretty blonde last night…and Michael mentioned you weren't home this morning."

As his grandmother's butler, Michael not only took care of the house but kept Gran informed of what everyone was doing, Dare suspected.

"We hit it off," Dare said. "She's nice. She was dumped by her boyfriend, so she crashed the reception. I wasn't sure what her motives were at first, so I kept her close."

"And things developed?" she asked.

He tipped his head to the side, arching one eyebrow at her. "You know a gentleman never talks."

She laughed. "I'm glad to hear that. And to see you smiling. I worry about you down in DC."

"Why?" he asked.

"You're too kind for that type of cutthroat maneuvering."

"I do it pretty well," he reminded her.

"I know but I think it takes a toll. That's why I'm happy to see you, well, happier this morning."

"Thanks, Gran. I am, too. What about you? What will you do when we all leave?" he asked.

"Breathe."

He laughed again. "Are you ready for some alone time?"

"Definitely. Obviously, I love you all, but I will be happy tonight when it's just me, Michael and my cocktail."

"I can understand that. Like you said, I'm looking forward to being back in my own place."

"I will miss you. I'm going to be down in DC for a gallery opening later this summer, I'll let you know my schedule so we can have dinner."

"I'll look forward to it," he said, kissing her cheek and standing as it was almost time to head to the heliport and leave Nantucket.

"Will the blonde be there?" she asked.

"Sadly, no."

"Ah, that is sad. But at least she made you smile for a bit," Gran said. "Bye, Dare."

"Bye, Gran," he said. "Love you."

"I love you, too, my boy."

He left his grandmother and headed to the heliport. The entire time he tried not to dwell on the question his grandmother had asked. Would he see Melody again? He knew that the answer was no, and he'd felt fine about it when he'd left her but now he was thinking more and more about her. Wondering if he shouldn't have gotten her last name or contact info. Even just a social media handle. There was no reason why casual had to be for one night only, was there?

His sister, Marielle, and her fiancé, Inigo Velasquez, were waiting for Dare at the heliport. They were a welcome distraction from his thoughts about Melody.

"We were about to leave without you," Mari said, putting her hand on her hip. "Inigo has to fly off to his next race and I don't like it when he goes."

"I know," he said, waving to Inigo and kissing his sister on the cheek. "I had to say goodbye to Gran."

"Oh, well, I guess that's okay, then. I hope she won't be too lonely once we're all gone."

"I think she'll be fine," Dare said.

"She'll probably just sit and enjoy the quiet," Inigo said.

"What are you saying?"

"That your family is loud, and this weekend hasn't been easy."

"Fair enough," Mari said. "I'm just glad I wasn't the one causing trouble. I was tempted to send a group text to the family and say we needed a meeting to talk about the dad problem. Just to point out that it wasn't the M problem for a change."

Dare laughed at his sister's comment. She was the youngest in their family and had been known for her partying ways and her reputation as a troublemaker. More than once the Bissets' public relations advisor, Carlton Mansford, would text the family to discuss "the M problem." So, Dare totally got where she was coming from, but he knew his father wouldn't have found it funny.

"I'm glad you didn't," Inigo said. "I think your father would have gone ballistic."

"That might have been better than the apologetic, humble guy he's been for the last couple days. I feel like he's bottling up all of his emotions and is going to explode," Mari said.

Dare wasn't too sure what his dad was going to do once they were all back home and he didn't have the public to play to. It reminded Dare of what Melody had said the night before about how her mom wouldn't tolerate her father cheating like August had. He made a mental note to reach out to both of his parents next week and check in on them.

He knew he had no control over his birth order but there were times he felt it would be nice not to be the eldest. He worried over his siblings, and as his parents had gotten older, he worried over them. This situation was the biggest his parents had faced in decades. Dare knew his mom had forgiven August for his infidelity so many times in the past, but would she be able to do it again?

And if she didn't, how would his father cope?

The other side of the coin was Juliette's revelation about Logan. That she'd swapped him in the hospital for her own stillborn child with none other than Cora Williams, who'd given birth to twins. That Logan was Nick Williams's twin, no less! A twin born of the infidelity between August and Cora.

Dare's father had always loved Juliette but this old wound might prove too deep for them to recover from.

Which simply made Dare realize that it was a good thing he hadn't gotten Melody's number; he certainly didn't trust himself in a relationship with anyone he cared about.

Melody's office was a small, cramped space in what could charitably be called the lower level of the building. There were three desks shoved into the space that she shared with Aubrey and Chris, the other full-time researchers on staff. All three of them seemed to be of the same mindset. Do whatever it took to get out of the basement and up into the plate glass windowed offices with a view. Or at least that was Melody's impression.

Chris and Aubrey were still putting the finishing touches on their presentations for this morning's research meeting, but she'd had hers finished since she got to work. She was sort of at loose ends waiting for them to finish up and for the clock to get to 10:00 a.m. when the meeting with her boss started.

She opened her internet browser and did a search on Darien Bisset. Of course, the newsfeed on him showed photos from the weekend wedding but the stories were mainly focused on the shock news that August Bisset was really Nick Williams's biological father. She clicked on one of the headlines, which linked to a story accompanied by a photo of Dare taken the day of the wedding.

She remembered how that custom-made suit jacket had fit his shoulders and how the stubble on his jaw had felt against her skin.

"Melody? You ready to head upstairs?" Chris asked from behind her.

"Yeah, I am."

"I thought you were done with your research?" he asked.

"I am. Was just double-checking that nothing new has come up," she said, minimizing her browser and closing her laptop as she stood. She made sure her skirt fell neatly to her just above her knees and took a quick glance down her body to ensure that her blouse was still neatly tucked in and then pulled on her suit jacket.

The political arena was definitely one where she had to dress for success. She noticed both Aubrey and Chris checking their looks in the full-length mirror they'd hung over the back of their office door. In another situation, they'd probably be friends. But they were totally driven, type-A personalities, and competition was always going to keep them from truly trusting each other.

"Let's go wow 'em," Chris said.

Melody hid a smile as they filed out of the office. She'd had a professor who used to say that exact same thing. She'd aced that class and felt confident that today she was going to wow her boss.

Johnny Rosemond had started his career in the early 2000s as a pharmaceutical rep and transitioned into working with one of the largest lobbying groups in the country. He then opened his own firm five years ago. He was one of the most powerful men in the country and he didn't hesitate to use his clout to get what he wanted. Melody, her fellow researchers and the interns they managed were the cream of the crop and were all positioning themselves to follow in his footsteps.

"Okay, team. What have we got?" Johnny asked, rubbing his hands together as he gestured for them to come into his office. "I hope you have something good, because so far no one seems to be willing to put their money where their mouth is with Bisset. Between his family's long reach in politics and his own reputation for being a man of his word…well, he's a tough nut."

Melody looked at Chris and Aubrey, ready to go first, but Aubrey beat her to it. She presented her findings and ideas for pursuing further research leads, which were pretty basic, and Melody just listened in case there was some new nugget of intel she could add to her dossier. Chris went next, and again she listened, ready to add any new information he had. But there wasn't anything.

"You have anything different from these two?" Johnny asked, looking at her. Aubrey and Chris hadn't found anything too groundbreaking in their reports and honestly if she hadn't crashed Dare's cousin's wedding, hers would sound the same.

"Yes, I do. I learned that Bill Turnball is working both sides of the issue and has been trying to set up a meeting with Bisset. I think if we get to him first, we can leverage that before we meet with the senator. Also, Senator Bisset is just like Aubrey and Chris have mentioned. He's loyal, and considers himself a man of his word, so he'll honor whatever he agrees to. I think that Turnball is the way to go in order to get the jump."

"How do you know this?" Johnny asked.

Melody sat there for a minute; she definitely didn't want to say she'd had a sneak peek at Dare's phone. "I know someone who works in Representative Hank Cooper's office and they mentioned it. I thought it might be a useful lead and did some digging. I've included everything I found in my presentation. I wanted to set up a meeting but thought I should wait for your go-ahead first."

Johnny pulled her presentation to him and started reading it. She noticed his senior staff were making notes and it wasn't long before Johnny finished and looked over at her.

"This is good. Shawna, make an appointment with Bill Turnball and then with Hank Cooper." Shawna was Johnny's assistant and the most senior person on their team. "Melody, since you dug most of this up, I want you there. We need to be focused on getting the exact information that will win Bisset over to our side. Chris and Aubrey, thanks for your reports. I'll see you both tomorrow for our update meeting. Melody, please stay so we can discuss this further."

Yes!

She watched the researchers leave and the last vestiges of that guilt-like feeling she'd been having left her. This was why she'd taken the risk and crashed the wedding reception, and it was paying off.

She spent the rest of the day in the conference room working with Johnny's A-team. He gave her assignments to farm out to the interns and then had her make calls to gather more information for the meetings with both Turnball and Representative Cooper. She was also invited to lunch with Johnny, where they brainstormed a plan to maneuver Dare's committee into making the decision they needed them to make.

In short, it was her dream afternoon, and though she hadn't totally stopped feeling guilty about how she'd gotten the scoop on her coworkers, she was glad she had done it. This was what she'd been working hard for. Too bad she didn't have anyone to share it with.

She felt pretty good until the meeting ended and Johnny looked over at her. "I really like what you've done here, Melody. I want you with me when we go to talk with Senator Bisset. I'll have Shawna put it on your calendar."

Waves of shock rolled over her. She was a researcher. She hadn't anticipated she'd be in a meeting with Dare. This would be awkward. And might cost her the job she'd just worked so hard to get.

Being back at work hadn't stopped Dare from thinking about Melody. He loved his offices in the Capitol Building, where he had a small dedicated staff. In addition to being an interim committee chair, he was sponsoring or cosponsoring several bills. Lobbying reform was one of his pet projects, and in this area, he was having some success reaching across the aisle to reach bipartisan consensus that everyone was interested in. To his way of thinking, it cost both sides and the taxpayers a lot of money when Congress only served the interest of big business and not the people. And lobbyists had a big part of the blame for that.

He was trying to stay focused, but the truth was he'd been distracted, and not just by Melody. Something had changed while he was at Nantucket. A big part of it was how he looked at his parents. There were things about them he'd always known and accepted, but suddenly it felt as if he didn't know these people at all. His mother's deception in hiding the truth of who Logan was had hit everyone hard. Dare could remember when Logan had first come home with his mom from the hospital. For a short while after that, maybe a few years, the four of them had been a pretty solid family. So Dare understood why she'd lied about Logan being her child—to keep the peace with August. Shocking as it was, to her thinking, having a healthy child would tie August to her and keep him from straying. But after a while, it hadn't been enough for Dare's father.

He'd gone back to work and his affairs, and every time his mom found out and the two of them made up, Dare would have another brother nine months later. He wondered sometimes why the two of them kept at the marriage. Why not just end things and go their own separate ways?

But they hadn't. And that upbringing had shaped Dare. He never wanted that kind of merry-go-round in his personal life again. Steering clear of commitment had been the best approach.

So why was his mind on Melody? A woman he'd never see again was haunting his dreams and making him question his long-held beliefs.

"Johnny Rosemond and his team have requested a meeting this afternoon to discuss some things before you go to committee. I told him your calendar was full, but I'd see what we could do," Cami Osteen said. She was thirty-two and had been his chief of staff for the last eight years. She had thick curly hair she wore in a short pixie cut. She worked and played hard and wasn't afraid to go toe to toe with some of the old dogs that had been in the Senate forever.

"I wonder what he's up to," Dare said. "He knows that we can't discuss anything privately and not share it with the committee."

"He does. But apparently they have some information that they think we will find helpful."

Hmm. He wondered what Johnny had. "Set up the meeting."

"Great. Also, Tim Kramer wants a meeting," she said.

"Of course, he does." Tim was the leader of a social watchdog group who was determined to use Dare's committee to take a swipe at big business and their lobbyists. While Dare admired his passion, his methods weren't always ones he could get behind. "I'm tempted to meet with him and Johnny at the same time. Those two like a good fight. They're both trying to steer us toward the result they want."

"They definitely are. Should I put them on back-to-back?"

He shook his head. "As fun as that might be for us, it would also piss them both off. No, put Johnny on today and Tim tomorrow."

"Sounds good," she said. "We have to pick some interns for the fall. I put the profiles on your desk and we also need a new assistant in the New York office. Larry and his husband are expecting their first child and Larry wants to stay home."

"That's great news for them," he said. He jotted a line in his planner to call Larry and Bob and send them a gift. He'd miss Larry, who was more than just an assistant. He was good at organizing events and keeping the office running smoothly while Dare was in DC. "I don't know if one person can handle all of Larry's responsibilities. Will you see if he can help in the interview process?"

"He already thought of that and sent you a list of candidates that he found in a search on the job sites. He also recommended we think of promoting J.J."

Leave it to Larry to give them more notice than was required and find people who could replace him. He was the kind of staffer that Dare knew most people wanted but rarely found. "Of course, he did. It's in that pile?"

He pointed to the stack that Jamie had dumped on his desk earlier.

"Yup. How was the wedding?" she asked. "I hated to bail on being your date."

"That's okay. I found someone to fill in."

"You did?" she asked.

"Yes. And that's all I'm going to say."

"Fair enough," Cami said. "I found someone this weekend, too."

"Who?"

"I can't say." She winked at him as she left his office and closed the door behind her.

He pulled the stack of résumés she'd left for him closer and looked at the Post-it note with "Interns" written on it. He wondered how old Melody was. She'd said she was just out of law school, just like these applicants. So midtwenties, tops.

Which was fine, because he'd already decided that she wasn't for him. He wasn't seeing her again. But the age difference would matter if she hadn't been a one-night stand.

He got out of the office to clear his head. He

glanced at his watch, noticing it was lunch time. Coming around the corner to a café, he thought he saw her. It was just from the back but he remembered her curves. He started after her but one of his aides caught up with him and he dismissed it. She was on his mind today, but even though she worked in DC, the chances of her being near his offices was slim.

Maybe he'd try to find her number. He couldn't stop thinking about her. But then what? She was younger than him; he'd done the right thing by walking away from her. And she'd clearly wanted him to go.

He put her out of his mind throughout the afternoon while he was in meetings and on calls. Jamie let him know that Johnny Rosemond and his team were in the conference room. He went to join them, opening the door and stopping as he saw Melody standing there facing him. Their eyes met and she flushed and sort of nodded at him.

He saw the rest of Johnny's team, three other professionals who all turned as he entered and smiled at him. He shook each of their hands and kept his politician smile firmly in place. But inside anger started to simmer.

She'd used him.

He knew he'd made it easy for her to do so but seeing her here made him realize that she'd had ulterior motives for crashing the reception after all. He just hadn't asked the right questions. A mistake he wouldn't make again.

Five

"Let me introduce my team. This is Paul Deville, Constance Kipling and Melody Conner," Johnny said to Dare as he came into the room.

She braced herself for him to expose her and possibly say that she'd snuck into his cousin's wedding, which would be totally fair. She was ready to resign her job and walk away when Dare told Johnny how they'd met. But he didn't. And when he shook her hand that familiar tingle went through her. He held her hand longer than the others and when their eyes met she realized that her research hadn't been as thorough as she'd thought.

Because until that moment she hadn't gotten a glimpse of Dare's anger. But it was cold and calm. She could see the rage in his eyes and had the feeling that it might be better if he just exposed her to Johnny and had her removed from the meeting.

Which he didn't do.

Instead he conducted the meeting with a genial civility that she realized reminded her a lot of how his mother had been at the wedding reception. Melody now understood how he'd been raised to function on two levels. The social level, where his feelings were imperceptible because of the expected norms, and then on another level, where he reacted with his true emotions.

She looked at Johnny and the others but they didn't seem to notice anything other than Dare's affability. Was she just picking up on it because of her secret connection to Dare? Or did sleeping with him once give her some insight she hadn't realized?

She wasn't too sure but when she noticed both Dare and Johnny looking at her, she knew she had to start paying attention in the meeting. "I'm sorry, could you repeat that?"

"Johnny mentioned you'd been in touch with Bill Turnball and he spoke to you about his position as a special advisor to the committee," Dare said.

"Yes, I know someone who had mentioned it in passing. No details, we just did some digging around and found out more," she said carefully, knowing that Dare would guess she'd read it on his phone if she said she'd gotten her info from Representative Cooper.

Dare nodded and she wondered if he was drawing

a line straight back to that text he'd received. She realized suddenly that as much as she liked winning, she might have crossed a line she didn't even realize she had. She also realized that she was starting to feel sick to her stomach.

She'd always thought that there was nothing she wouldn't do to win, but now, having done this, she wasn't sure she would ever be able to do it again. She wanted to reassure herself that at least now she knew her limits, but it was hard to do that while the conversation swirled around her. She felt the career advantage she'd gained by being assigned to this team slipping away because she wasn't focusing.

She pulled her notepad closer and refused to look over at Dare again. She was going to be a top member of the team dealing with his committee and now she had some new information about Dare that she could factor in.

That cold anger that she could feel even from her position down the table from him.

Johnny was talking as he did, laying out some really good, solid facts that would show Dare that his advisor was playing both sides, and she could see that Dare was happy to have the information. She was pretty sure it was how Johnny got that information that was bothering him.

The meeting wrapped up after forty-five minutes. Dare's assistant asked for their numbers and emails so she could send the meeting notes to them later. Melody didn't have cards, so Johnny handed her one of his and told her to jot her information on it, which she did as the rest of the party walked out of the room with Dare, still talking.

She had never felt so out of her depth as when she looked up to hand the card to Dare's assistant and she gave her an encouraging smile.

"First job?"

"Yeah. It is."

"You must be good to be in this meeting," the assistant said.

Melody really wished she hadn't let Dare rattle her, so she could remember this woman's name. Her dad would be embarrassed by her lack of manners, she thought. Plus it was just good business sense to remember names.

"Thanks. I was a little nervous when we came in. I don't remember your name," she admitted.

"It's Cami Osteen," she said. "I was a complete wreck when I started in this office, so I get it."

Cami.

This was the woman who was supposed to have been Dare's date at the reception. If she'd been there, Melody wondered if she'd have even met him. Cami was attractive and smart and it would be easy to see her and Dare as a couple. Of course, they worked together so they probably weren't.

She didn't know why she even cared. She'd slept with Dare because it had been part of the night and that was it. Nothing more. It didn't matter that she'd been thinking about him ever since. The sex had been hot, so of course she wasn't going to forget it.

But that was it.

She walked out of the conference room and found Dare standing there alone. "Ms. Conner, I told your team to go ahead. I'll see you down to meet them."

"Thank you. I'm sure I won't have any problem finding them," she said. She definitely didn't want to be alone with Dare right now. He needed to calm down before they spoke alone again...so maybe in a decade or so.

"I insist," he said, putting his hand under her elbow and walking her toward the door of his offices. His grip on her arm told her that he wasn't going to let her get away without talking to her.

He led the way to the elevators, and when they got inside, he used his key card to stop it.

"Melody," he said. "Want to tell me what you were really doing at my cousin's wedding?"

Dare leaned in, cornering her in the elevator car. He was pissed. No matter how he tried to view her actions, she'd used him and played him for a fool. And he was beginning to wonder why he hadn't seen it. Was he losing his touch?

Hell, no.

He hadn't ever let himself be played and he wasn't about to let Melody get away with it now. Except it wasn't hard to see why he'd been so easily duped.

Tonight he was getting the perfectly polished version of Melody he'd first encountered at the wedding reception. His gut had told him she had an ulterior motive to seek out his family, he'd just been too distracted by his parents' scandals to think it could be him she was after.

She wore a pencil skirt that ended just above her knees and hugged her hips. Her blouse was tucked in and accentuated her tiny waist. He could see the birthmark behind her left ear that he'd licked when they'd had sex.

He was thinking about taking her into his arms and kissing her hard. Making her understand that she had no power over him. That despite the fact that he'd slept with her and she'd used him, he was still in control.

But he knew that he wasn't. That he had to somehow wrest power back from her. And being a Bisset he knew how to do it. But honestly, he'd never gone there in the past. Would Melody be the woman who pushed him past his own internal barriers? The safety guards he kept in place to keep from giving in to the animalistic, do-anything-to-win man that his father was?

She tucked a strand of her hair behind her ear and arched one eyebrow at him as she said, "I saw an opportunity and I took it," she said. "I heard that you were going to be on Nantucket and decided to meet you and do some research."

"Research? I'm not sure what I look like naked

is something that is going to help you or Johnny in the committee hearings."

"It might," she said, putting her hand on his chest, and a tingle went through him, which he ignored because he was still mad. He wanted payback. She owed him.

She'd used him and smiled while she'd done it.

Had he simply not expected it because she'd seemed so genuine? She was a better actor than he'd given her credit for.

"I doubt that. I've slept with Constance and believe me she isn't going to be swayed by any details you might add," Dare said. Of course, he and Constance had been congressional interns at the time and both had been a little drunk. It had been a long time ago.

"Well, then I don't see why you're upset with me," she said, ducking under his arm and moving across the elevator car. "It seems this kind of thing is normal for you."

He doubted that anything about this was normal for him or for her. But maybe it was normal. Was this just one step closer to being like his father? He didn't know and really didn't care at this moment.

"It was just sex," he said. Watching to see how she reacted.

She smiled at him. "Exactly. No need to make a big deal about it."

He nodded. She was cool. He hadn't really expected anything else from her since the moment she'd appeared in his office with Johnny. But the woman he'd met at the reception, who'd videotaped Toby Osborn to send to her mom…she'd seemed like a different woman. Someone too genuine and sincere to be this calculating.

"Glad to hear that. So what exactly were you fishing for?" he asked. Because he was pretty sure she'd found out about Turnball from his phone. At the time he hadn't thought anything of his clothing being moved to the table from the floor in her hotel room, but now he wondered if she'd somehow accessed his phone.

"Information. I just wanted to get to know the enemy…not that we are enemies," she said quickly. "We aren't adversaries. We both want this bill to affect as many people as possible and change lives. Researching you was a way to help me help the team reach that objective. This is my first big job and I wanted to go in with as much knowledge as I could."

Knowledge. He sort of respected her for seeing the opportunity and taking it. He had done the same thing more than once in his career, but he'd never been the one who felt…like this. Like he'd been played. He couldn't let it go. Maybe it was because he hadn't been able to stop thinking how it had felt to have her arms and legs wrapped around him.

That was sexual, and he'd never been truly comfortable with the more animalistic side of his nature. "So you're saying sleeping with me had nothing to do with you working for Johnny?"

"Obviously I didn't plan to sleep with you," she said. "There was just something there when we touched and I wanted you. You wanted me, too. Seemed silly not to do something about it."

"What if I said I still wanted you?" he asked, moving closer.

She put her hand up. "It would depend on whether you thought I was sleeping with you to get information."

"Would you be?" he asked.

She nibbled her lower lip and he felt like he could almost feel her weighing her options. "I can't just straight-out say no. If you say something I can use, I won't be able to unhear it. I don't want to lie to you again."

"At least you admit to lying."

"Of course, I do. I wasn't planning to stay or to even meet you, but things happened and there I was sitting at your family table," she said.

"Fair enough. That's on me. But going forward you should know that information flows both ways," he said.

"Of course it does," she admitted. "What are you getting at?"

What was he getting at?

He wanted her. He hadn't been lying about that. He knew that if he didn't do something about the attraction between them, he'd be distracted every time she came into his offices. He also knew from the past that the longer he denied himself something the bigger the obsession became. Maybe sleeping with her now that he knew the truth would be all it took for him to get over Melody, stop waking up with a hard-on in the middle of the night and reaching for her when she wasn't there.

"I want to continue our affair, unless you can't handle it."

Melody watched him carefully. Since he'd stopped the elevator car she was very aware of Dare the man. She'd definitely not thought of him as Senator Bisset in the time they'd been in here. His aftershave brought back memories of their one night together and reminded her of what it had been like to be held in his arms.

His words were a verbal gauntlet. Her gut said to pick it up and take his challenge but her mind for once was urging caution. Was there something she was missing?

Already she felt guilty about her actions on Nantucket. Not sleeping with him but looking at his phone, using that information to get ahead. And then there was the fact that Cami was supposed to be Dare's date at the wedding. She was much more suited to being with Dare than Melody herself was. Or was she? Dare was asking her to continue things and she wasn't going to fool herself. He wasn't looking for a little bit of revenge on her.

She'd gotten one over on him. She'd been raised in a competitive environment so she knew he'd want to even the score. She also was pretty sure she could hold her own with him. It was her emotions that had her concerned for the first time ever. She'd almost lost her focus—hell, who was she kidding, she'd completely lost it while she'd been seated across the boardroom table from Dare.

Could she keep that from happening again?

Maybe if they were sleeping together then she wouldn't be as distracted as she'd been today. That made sense, right? Also, she wouldn't be lying to him anymore, so he'd know the score. And so would she.

"I can handle it," she said sardonically. "Can you?"

"I think I'll manage," he said, moving closer to her.

Earlier when he'd leaned over her after stopping the elevator, she knew he'd been trying to intimidate her but honestly he'd just turned her on.

It felt like for the first time since they'd been in bed together she was seeing the real man. Dare was used to smiling and playing politics, not just in DC but in his real life as well. She'd observed that from the first moments they'd met, when he was smiling and trying to get her out of the reception before she ruined his cousin's big day.

However, that wasn't who he truly was. He hid behind those manners and his family's reputation, pretending to be someone who was used to maneuvering in scandal. But she suspected he didn't like it.

And as he came closer to her, moving like a tiger who had found something new and different and wasn't sure how to approach his prey, but at the same time wasn't about to back down, she knew she wanted him. She liked the way he made her feel. Like it was okay to be aggressive and go after the things she wanted. Like she didn't have to hide who she truly was from him.

Which couldn't be true. He was a senator and she worked for a lobbyist. There were going to be times when they weren't on the same page. No matter how she wanted to pretty it up he wasn't going to suddenly not be a senator in control of making a decision that was going to affect her job. If she slept with him then it could only be for the sex and maybe for some information he might leak.

But she was pretty sure he'd be very careful not to let anything slip again. She'd probably gotten all the information she could from Dare. But at the same time, her body wasn't done with him.

She was a sophisticated woman. Not a college student anymore, she reminded herself. She could handle an affair with Dare. She wanted an affair with Dare.

He was so close now that she could feel his body heat, and as he leaned down, his minty breath brushed over her cheek.

"What if I manage you?" she asked cheekily.

"I'm willing to let you try," he said. There was still that thin veil of him trying to be civilized, but when he touched her, he wasn't gentle or tentative. He put his hand on her waist and pulled her to him. His mouth came down on hers, taking the kiss he wanted, and a part of her knew that he was getting back some of his pride.

He kissed her deeply, demanding she meet his passion, and she had no problem doing that. She put her hands on the sides of his neck and rose on her tiptoes to take more of his mouth. To thrust her tongue deeper until he ripped his head back. His nostrils flared with each inhalation of breath and his lips were wet from their kiss. He watched her with hungry eyes.

"I can't do this here," he said.

"Why not?"

"The risk of discovery is too high," he said. "I usually run the Mall after work around six."

"I can do that," she said. "I live in Crystal City."

"I have a place we can go," he said. "Are you sure about this? I don't want to hurt you."

"What about you? Won't you get hurt?" she asked. Why did he think the risk was higher for her? Was it that he doubted she could balance having an affair with doing her job?

"No, I won't. I'm a Bisset. We don't fall in love," he said.

She'd disagree with that, having seen his brother fawning all over Iris Collins at the reception, but she knew he was warning her. He wasn't going to be some sort of knight in shining armor. The thing was, she'd never needed one, so that worked for her.

"Then we should both be good," she said, reaching around him to put the elevator car back in motion. "See you at six."

She pulled out her compact and fixed her lipstick. When the doors opened, she walked away from him without a backward glance.

Six

Dare changed into his running clothes and donned a Moretti Racing baseball cap that Inigo had sent him along with some other swag. Bailey, his eight-year-old Saint Bernard, was already waiting for him in the hallway with his leash in his mouth.

"Hey, boy, ready to go?" he asked, as he took the leash and clipped it onto Bailey's collar. The dog licked his hand and then moved toward the door.

Dare lived in a newish town house near the Potomac, a little over a mile from the Mall, which was just right for his run. He could have just gone to the gym in his development, but he liked to exercise outside. He had a better chance of hearing what everyday people were talking about and he liked to keep in touch with that. He had been elected to make policy and he couldn't do that if he was out of touch.

He'd already made the decision to retire from politics after two terms in the Senate because he thought that to effect real change, Congress should have fresh blood.

And he wanted to explore some other things. Honestly, he'd been thinking more and more of starting a think tank. He'd seen his father and Logan use government policies to their advantage at Bisset Industries and he wanted to make that sort of access to government more available for smaller businesses. Now that he was serving his second term in the Senate, he only had a few years to finalize those plans.

Family had always seemed like something else he might explore someday but those dreams were fading. He definitely wasn't looking for family now as he started something with Melody. Something that felt exciting and a little bit forbidden, given her job.

Also he'd always been careful not to be involved with anyone or anything that could be construed as currying favor. Even with his own relatives, who often tried to lobby for legislation. But he knew that this thing with Melody was partially motivated by revenge and the need to get back his own after she'd played him.

But she'd made the decision to continue the affair with him. His conscience was clear. He wasn't going to do anything unethical as far as his job was concerned.

He turned to enter the Mall and realized that he hadn't specified where exactly they should meet in the vast space. Had he been too vague when he'd told her he jogged at the Mall? But then he saw her.

She wore running clothes and a pair of cat's-eye-shaped black sunglasses, and had her blond hair in a high ponytail. She waved when she saw him.

"Good to see you," he said, stopping to give Bailey a drink from the water bottle he'd carried with him.

"Who's this?" she asked, bending down and holding her hand out for Bailey to sniff it.

Dare forced himself not to stare at her ass, but it was difficult to tear his gaze from her. "Bailey."

"Hello, Bailey," she said, scratching behind the dog's ears.

Bailey was immediately smitten with Melody and licked her hand when she stood up.

"So, why do you run here?" she asked.

He shrugged and started walking on the large grassy area away from the crowds. Melody kept pace at his side.

"It's a good place to keep up with what's on people's minds," he said. "What about you?"

"I don't jog normally," she said. "I have a Peloton in my apartment, and I use that."

"So you're here for me?" he teased.

"Originally. Now I think I might be here for Bailey. He's such a cutie," she said.

"He's a babe magnet and he knows it," Dare said.

"That's why you keep him around?" she asked.

"Nah, he's my buddy. I work long hours and travel between DC and New York a lot and he goes with me."

Dare wasn't about to say the dog was his best friend, but honestly there were times when it felt like that. Bailey was safe to talk to about whatever was on his mind. To be fair, Bailey had gotten an earful about Melody since Dare had picked him up at Cami's on Monday.

"Sounds great. I always wanted a dog but my brother has asthma and allergies and we couldn't risk it, so it wasn't an option growing up," she said.

Dare almost laughed at the way she said it. There was a tone of understanding but also a bit of resentment that he recognized from hearing Leo talk about Logan. As if her brother had that health condition on purpose to keep her from getting a pet. It reminded him a lot of Leo and Logan and how they interacted with each other. "You could get one now."

"I could," she said. "I have a tiny apartment, so maybe not a dog as big as Bailey here."

Bailey wagged his tail when she said his name and Dare completely understood where his dog was coming from. Hearing Melody say his name made him happy, too. He wanted to pretend that she was like every other woman, but he knew she wasn't.

Which was why he needed to keep this just about sex. And when it came to lobbying before his committee, she was batting for the other team and not afraid to flirt with him until he missed the ball. He had to remember that. Had to remember she was the Melody who wanted something from him. He had to keep this about getting back a little of his ego. Use the lust between them to his advantage instead of letting her wrap him around her finger.

Which was harder than he thought it would be. He was used to keeping his cool around women but Melody had snuck past his radar, probably because he'd met her when he was in a social situation with his family. He'd been trying to keep his family safe and not thinking about himself.

"Ready for a run?" he asked. "I like to go to the Lincoln Monument and then we can get some ice cream."

"Try to keep up," she said, sprinting off ahead of him. Bailey started after her.

Dare kept pace with her and found that Melody wasn't one to let a challenge lie. He tucked that away, knowing he was going to use it to get that advantage he was looking for. She would always take a bet and he just had to figure out how to use that.

He promised himself he would as he ran next to her and then overtook her as they made their way through the crowds on this sultry DC evening.

Melody wasn't sure what to expect when she'd arrived at the Mall and looked around for Dare. Cami had told her he had a Saint Bernard, which had surprised Melody. He hadn't struck her as someone who'd be committed to anything but his job. How had she missed that? she thought as she ran along beside him. With her competitive streak, she knew she wasn't going to allow him to pull ahead of her at any point.

But she hadn't been lying when she said she wasn't a runner and her thirty minutes a day on the Peloton bike hadn't really prepared her for this run against Dare. It was clear to her from watching Bailey take the path ahead of them on his lead that he and Dare probably did this run at least once if not twice a day. So she kept her pace manageable until they got to the last park that led to the Lincoln Monument and then she put her head down and went for it.

She pushed herself harder than she had before, and she felt pretty darn good about it until first Bailey and then Dare zipped right past her. She tried to reach into the well of pain the way her high school swimming coach had taught her but it had been too long since she'd been in that kind of shape. She felt a stitch in her side as she forced herself to keep going to the end of the path and stop next to Dare and Bailey.

Dare gave the dog water from his water bottle first and then took some for himself. She put her hands on her knees and took a few deep breaths before standing up.

Dare watched her with one eyebrow lifted. "Water?"

"Do you have enough?" she asked. She hadn't brought a bottle with her but would the next time she ran. And she was definitely going to start running the Mall on a regular basis so that next time she wouldn't be beaten by Dare and his dog.

"Yeah. Plus, we get a refill when we get ice cream."

She took the bottle he offered and squirted some water into her mouth. Then she handed it back. "You keep saying we... How does Bailey eat ice cream?"

"In a bowl of course," Dare said, winking at her.

Despite herself she had to laugh. He was funny. And darn it, she liked him. She knew it wasn't wise to actually let herself go there because he was someone she was going to come up against a number of times in her career and they weren't always going to see eye-to-eye, no matter how she tried to frame it. Managing a purely sexual relationship with Senator Hottie was one thing. Actually starting to like the man was something else.

And she wanted to believe she was smarter than that.

After all, she'd used him and gotten caught at it. Given what she knew of Dare Bisset, he wasn't going to let that pass.

She had to remember that.

"Of course," she replied realizing that he was waiting for a response from her. "So do we get ice cream now or what?"

"We usually walk up to the Lincoln Monument and take a look at the inscriptions of the Gettysburg Address and Lincoln's second inaugural address. Remind ourselves of why we're here in DC," Dare said.

She looked over at him, not sure if he was joking, but she could see he was serious. She'd heard Johnny say that he had a lot of respect for Dare because he was well-liked on both sides of the aisle. The kind of politician that, if you asked Melody, only existed in movies or in theory. But she was starting to see pieces of that man now.

"Let's do it. I haven't been to the monument since I was twelve and on summer vacation with my family."

"I thought you went to Georgetown for college," he said.

"I did. It's a tough school. I didn't do anything but study for four years," she said, petting Bailey, who was bumping against her legs as the crowds got larger closer to the monument. There was a queue to get in and they took their place in line. A few people glanced at Dare as if they recognized him, but then looked away. Politicians weren't like rock stars who attracted fans who wanted selfies.

"I wish I'd been that studious. I'm lucky that I test well. Otherwise I would have been in big trouble."

"Did you party a lot?"

"Some. College was the first time that I was in a school that my dad didn't have any connections to."

"What do you mean?"

"All of the Bissets go to Winston Prep School. Dad's on the board of trustees and if I had stepped out of line he would have been up there in a heart-beat to make sure I was back on track. So I picked Berkeley for college because I would be far from my dad's influence. He didn't approve—in his words, it's a 'hippie' school."

She had to smile at the thought of Dare being at a hippie school, not that Berkeley really was a hippie school. Everything about him was American preppy and upper class, so it was hard to see him as a young rebel. But it was another interesting tidbit that…made her like him a bit more. Scrub that. It was a fact that she could use when they went in to present their arguments in front of the subcommittee. She was going to leverage everything she learned about him to score a win for her firm, and not allow herself to be swayed into liking him any more than she already did.

She kept telling herself that, and almost started to believe it, until he bought ice cream and they found a quiet spot on the grass for them to sit and eat it. He fed his dog first, and in that moment, Melody knew that not falling for Dare was going to be way harder than she'd expected it to be.

Bailey was on his best behavior, charming Melody easily. Dare could tell that she wasn't sure what to make of this meeting, and to be honest, he really wasn't, either. It wasn't as if he were some kind of villain in a black-and-white movie who was going to demand some kind of sexual favor in return for her playing him at the reception.

In fact, he liked her more than he wanted to. Not too surprising, given that she was smart, sassy and competitive. He'd known from the moment they met that there was more to Melody than met the eye.

But seeing her with Johnny today had made him realize that he couldn't forget this was DC and she was in the political game. He had to remember what his mentor had told him a long time ago: politics was perception. He couldn't afford to give her the impression that she'd bested him.

So he was showing off with his dog and talking about the city that he truly loved. There was a lot to hate about politics and those who played the game with an agenda, but he'd gotten into it because he loved this country and wanted to make it a better place for everyone.

Bailey finished his ice cream way before the humans were done. As Dare leaned back on his elbow watching her lick her ice cream and getting turned on, he knew he needed to establish some parameters. If not for her then definitely for himself.

"I know I was a little aggressive today in the elevator and I'm sorry about that," he said. "I let my... temper get the better of me."

"Apology accepted," she said. "I'm not sure I wouldn't have reacted the same way if the tables were turned. I'm sorry for not coming clean about who I was when we met. It's just that in politics it does seem like it's a game of three-card monte."

He hadn't heard it put that way before but he definitely knew what she meant. There was a lot of sleight of hand in DC and he had been guilty of using those tactics to get what he wanted as well. "The ends justify the means. Is that how you think of your job?"

"Yes," she said. "I try to operate within my own moral code but at the end of the day if I can get the results that Johnny and our team want then I will go for it."

Interesting. "So does that go both ways, then? I can use the same tactics?"

"Of course. You can't truly play to win unless it's a level playing field for everyone. There aren't two sets of rules."

"I agree. That's part of why I became a senator. I wanted to change policies to make the world fairer. Which is also why I am on this committee. I'm tired of seeing people forced to decide between putting food on the table or getting medicine that can treat a chronic illness. This was never an issue for my family but not everyone has my means."

"I get it. But just because someone has money doesn't mean they are evil," she said. "I think this is the kind of issue that strikes close to home for a lot of congressmen and women. But it does cost money to develop and manufacture these new life-saving drugs. A lot of the companies we represent have rebates that are aimed at those very people you want to help. I think it's safe to say that we will have to go after the vote to keep you from passing your bill as it is written."

"So where exactly does that leave us?" he asked.

"Because I don't see you as the type of woman to back down and I know I'm not the kind of man who will."

She finished her ice cream cone and then cleaned her hands with her napkin before pushing her sunglasses up on her head. She had pretty brown eyes and up close he could see flecks of gold in them. "I don't know. I like you, Dare, but I don't want to do anything that would reflect badly on my career or yours. I know I was out of line at the reception. To be fair, I never thought I'd be in the meeting with you, but still that isn't an excuse."

He thought about her words. There was a danger only if one of them revealed some strategy that they were using to get votes. This entire thing would be over by November. So it was basically three months of possibly dating this woman who was turning him on with every little thing she did, or ignoring his lust until the vote was over.

"Are we both the kind of people who can keep work at the office?" he asked. "That's really what we have to know. I'm willing to give this a chance because I haven't been able to stop thinking about that one night we had together. A part of me is convinced that it was too short and if we did it again, then I'd be able to move on."

"Only a part of you?" she teased.

"The other part thinks it's foolish to tempt fate," he admitted. He'd never been one for playing games with the opposite sex; he'd seen the way that had played out with his parents and somehow neither of them ever seemed to truly win.

"Fate? I'm not sure I believe in fate," she said. "But I do like the idea of hooking up again, seeing if that takes care of this attraction... What do you say? One more night together?"

One more night together.

She made it sound so simple. Damn. She made him very aware of the difference in years and experience between the two of them with that statement. He knew that sex and emotions and politics were never a simple combination. And the attraction between them was strong enough that they both seemed willing to ignore the red flags.

He should be the mature one and put a stop to it, yet at the same time, he wanted her. She'd used him the first time and he knew that despite his earlier apology about being too aggressive he still needed to take her again to assuage that beast inside of him. The one who didn't like being tricked or fooled.

"That works for me," he said realizing that no matter what his feelings for her were after they hooked up again, he had to end this.

Seven

Dare's town house was modern and clean. Very clean. It had an open floor plan and a large window with a view of an enclosed patio behind the building.

When they arrived, Bailey trotted to his water bowl and drank while Dare set out his dinner. When Bailey was finished eating, the dog settled on his blanket next to the built-in fireplace.

Melody sat on one of the bar stools while Dare prepped for their meal. When he'd invited her to have dinner with him, she wasn't sure what she'd expected. Maybe for him to order takeout or something along those lines.

"I've already prepped some chicken for a Greek pasta bowl," he said. "Well, I didn't prep it, my housekeeper did. But if you're vegetarian I can swap in some marinated artichoke hearts."

"I'm not veggie," she said. "So your housekeeper prepped this? I was really impressed that you had your meal all planned."

"Really? Sometimes I do the planning myself," he said.

"What do your meal plans look like?"

He winked at her. "A bowl of two-minute rice and some protein that I heat up in the microwave. Chicken, teriyaki beef or tofu. That kind of thing. When Helena realized what I was eating every night she was horrified."

Melody laughed as she knew he expected her to. He'd kept up a running conversation since they'd left the Mall and walked back to his place. She liked it. It was almost as if they were two random people who'd met and decided to date. And she wished that were true. Because he was funny and real. So many guys she met were trying to be someone they weren't. Everyone in DC was working an agenda and relentlessly moving forward. But Dare was just being Dare.

And she liked it—liked him—more than she wanted to.

"She signed me up for a cooking class at Sur La Table," he continued. "I made Rashid and Cami come with me. Called it a team-building exercise, but honestly it was a lot of fun, and the few skills I learned have helped."

He turned on a grill pan and seared the chicken for a few minutes on each side. Then he assembled their Greek pasta bowls and passed a plate to her. "Normally I don't drink on work nights but you're here and it is our first date. So wine?"

Their first date.

She hadn't thought of it that way, and wasn't sure how the idea of a date with him made her feel. "Sure."

"Helena left a bottle of rosé to have with this. It's a nice summer wine," he said, pouring them both a glass.

Melody noticed that Helena had signed her note with an *H* and a heart. She suspected that Helena wanted to be more than Dare's housekeeper.

They ate their dinner on his enclosed patio. Over the course of the meal, Melody learned that he didn't like living in DC and preferred Manhattan, where he had a brownstone that had been in his family for generations.

"That must be nice. To live someplace where you know the history," she said.

"It is. And at the same time there is so much weight to being a Bisset. The brownstone is passed from grandparent to grandchild. My grandparents had seventeen properties in the tristate area and fourteen more scattered around the world. When I turned eighteen, Grandad asked me which one I wanted. I'm the oldest grandchild, so I got first choice. Mari is the youngest and she 'got stuck' with the ski cabin in Aspen."

"Got stuck?"

"Mari's way of putting it," he said.

"My family has a beach cottage in Martha's Vineyard that we share with my aunts and uncles," she said. "My family is pretty tight-knit—we all get along."

She and her brother were competitive, but she knew he'd have her back if she needed him, and her parents were always there for her even though they had high expectations of what she could achieve on her own. "Is your family supportive? I mean, from what I saw on the dance floor you all definitely closed ranks when it came to a dance-off with the Williams family."

He smiled. "I'd say we are supportive of each other most of the time. We will always unite against anyone on the outside, but we have our differences at times. Honestly, it's more Dad and Mom vs. me and my brothers and sister than a sibling rivalry thing. Logan and Leo go at it pretty hard sometimes but they both have very similar personalities."

"Isn't Logan only your half brother?" she asked. "Is it okay to ask that?"

"He is, but we never knew it growing up," Dare said. "I really don't want to discuss my parents or their issues."

"Fair enough," she said. She wouldn't want to talk about her parents, either, if they were dealing with the kind of secrets that his had been lately.

"Tell me about your parents," he said. "You mentioned they wouldn't be able to maintain a polite facade the way mine do when they're fighting."

"No. Let's just say in the Conner family if someone is mad at you the entire world will know it. We aren't much for subterfuge."

"That's not entirely true," he said, finishing off his glass of wine. "You were pretty shady with me when we first met."

He had a point. "But that's work. In real life I wouldn't be."

But would she? She was the first to admit she hadn't had a real relationship where she wasn't trying to get ahead in a long time, maybe ever.

"Your career is your real life," he said. "Am I your real life?"

What the hell was he doing? This was taking things further than he wanted to. But having her in his town house was making him…well, far more honest than he'd intended. But he didn't know any other way to be. He had one big lie between them. He wasn't going to be able to date her in public. Hell, he was his father's son, wasn't he, sneaking around with a woman he liked.

He wondered if the justifications he was using were at all similar to those that his father had used when he'd snuck around. Did it matter? Dare might not be cheating on women, but he was cheating as it were on his public image, and the end result was the same.

Deceit.

That seemed to be the Bisset trademark when it came to relationships.

Even his mother wasn't immune to doing it. Here he was grilling Melody on her deception when in reality she should be more concerned about the serial liar sitting next to her and his family's history of looking out for themselves over anyone else.

"I'm not sure what you are asking me," she said. "The job is pretty much my life. I mean I'm just starting out, so I can't do it halfway."

"I get it," he said. "Sorry for asking that. I can be a little too sassy sometimes."

He had been pushing to see what she was really doing here. Was he letting his hormones fool him into believing there was more of a connection than they had? It would be the first time in a long time that he'd done that. Maybe that was why…what? He wanted to demand answers from himself but he was in denial mode, enjoying her company. Or at least he had been until he'd pushed way too hard for something he wasn't ready to hear and she wasn't ready to give.

His phone pinged and he pulled it from his pocket. It was a text from Logan.

"Sorry. Not to be rude but it's my brother," he said.

"That's okay. I should check my emails as well. The team is getting an early start tomorrow," she said.

"Got to start trying to win votes from me, right?"

She shrugged. "That is how the game goes."

"Indeed."

She pulled her phone out and he glanced back at his. Logan was in deep water apparently.

Shit's hitting the fan with a deal I set up before the wedding. Can you talk?

Dare wasn't ready to let the night end. He hadn't been at his best before Logan had texted him.

"Hey. I need to talk to my brother, but I really don't want our date to end. Would you mind if I went inside and talked to him for a few minutes?" he asked her. If she said no, that was fine, but he hoped she wouldn't.

"Go ahead. I'm not ready for it to end, either. Can I have your Wi-Fi password? I need to download a file and my cell reception isn't that good here."

He shared his password and then went into the house, heading upstairs to the second bedroom that he'd set up as an at-home office. He closed the door behind him and dialed his brother.

"Thanks for calling," Logan said as he answered.

"No problem. What's up?"

"Um, I kind of sabotaged one of the Williams Inc.'s deals before the wedding and it's all coming out now. Even though I admitted it to Nick after the wedding and agreed to fix the problem, the press got wind of the story and are blowing it out of proportion. Nick and Adler are on their honeymoon but the rest of the Williams family is pissed at me and Dad and Tad are going after each other hard. I need some perspective."

"First of all, what is the deal? Is it a Bisset Industries thing?" he asked.

"No. I knew that Mom would be upset if I went after Nick but the bastard had just taken a big client out from under me. So I used a shell company to outbid him on a patent his company needs. It's a major coup that I won that auction, actually…"

"So congratulations," Dare said to lighten the tension he heard in his brother's voice.

Logan laughed. "Thanks. I mean it was a long shot. But it was totally motivated by hate and now that Nick and I are…well, now I know we're twins. And I want to fix this. The plan was to transfer the patent to his company. But now the press has gotten wind of the story and it's causing complications in the deal. Not to mention everyone in both families is mad at me—and Quinn is ticked, even though she knows the kind of man I am." Dare was still amazed at how Logan had reunited with his college sweetheart Quinn Murray during the wedding weekend, despite all the other chaos going on.

"Since Nick and Adler are away, maybe you can work with his father to fix the problem. Do you want me to talk to Tad Williams and explain the situation?" Dare asked. He'd always played the diplomat between the two families.

"Not really," Logan said. "But you have a point.

It might be better to get this taken care of before it becomes an even bigger issue. That way when Nick and Adler get home they can start their married life without this hassle. Nick thinks I'm taking care of it—he's in for a rude surprise."

"He shouldn't have to come home to another scandal," Dare said. "His father can represent their company to close this deal and get the patent transferred. I'll talk to him and smooth things over."

"You're right. Okay, do it."

"But I'm kind of on a date so it won't be until tomorrow—"

"You're on a date? Dare, you idiot, you shouldn't have called me."

"She understood," Dare said. "You needed me, Logan."

"I did and I appreciate it, but I know Quinn wouldn't be too pleased with me if she knew I was interrupting. Thank you, but go back to your girl."

"She's not mine yet," Dare admitted. And she probably would never be, Dare realized.

He said goodbye to his brother and went back downstairs to Melody, determined to figure out if he was wasting his time with her. Was this simply lust? God he hoped so. Because if not this might be a bigger mistake than his father's affair with Cora Williams all those years ago.

Melody wasn't too sure why she stayed, except as she'd said to Dare, she wasn't ready for the night to end. He'd gotten a bit too real for her before his brother had texted and it was making her think. She always stayed focused and tried not to let anything derail her, but his question earlier had thrown her off.

There was no way even in her wildest imagination that this night with Dare had anything to do with her career or the goals she was hoping to achieve. She was a lobbyist trying to stop a bill he wanted to get to the floor. They both were professionals adamant about their positions. Being intimate with him wouldn't change his mind.

Until now, she'd been having fun tonight. She had her guard up with Dare, but he also put her at ease, which was something she couldn't say about many men.

Wah-wah, she thought to herself. She hated when her mind went down the what-if path. But she was slowly realizing that Dare was a what-if scenario. What if she just let herself have this relationship with him? What if she stopped thinking about her career for one night and just let go? What if she stopped fighting this?

"Sorry about that," Dare said as he came back out onto the patio with two fresh drinks and Bailey, who came over and licked her leg.

"No problem. I assume you solved your brother's problems," she said, taking the glass he handed her.

"Not exactly. This is bigger than a ten-minute talk," he said. "There are times when I actually think it's easier to get both sides of Congress to agree on something than my family to work out their problems."

She laughed and took a sip of the drink he'd brought. "Families can be that way."

"But not yours," he said. "How do you handle things?"

"We obviously don't have as many players as you do," she said. "There's only four of us and if someone does something that reflects poorly on our family, we have a meeting—"

"Oh, we have those, too," he interrupted. "Ours include a spin doctor."

"Ours don't. Usually someone ends up having to apologize and then fix the thing they did that they knew was wrong."

"Sounds sensible. Logan's screwup is causing trouble with our family business and some tension in our cousin's marriage," Dare said. "That's just between us."

"I won't talk about it to anyone else. Is there anything I can do to help?"

"Not unless you are good at negotiation with hostile parties."

She actually was. It was the class she'd done the best in at college. "Um... I might be able to help. I worked at a prominent law firm through college under one of the best mediators in the country."

"Did you? What else have you done?"

"Mostly stuff like that. I was our debate team captain," she said.

"You like arguing," he pointed out.

"I do. Not irrational screaming at the top of my lungs stuff, but give me a topic and let me research it and I'll convince you to join my team," she said, wriggling her eyebrows at him.

"I can believe it. And it means I'm going to have to bring my A game if I'm going to keep you and your team from stopping my bill as written from passing."

"I'm sure you're up to the challenge," she said. "You look very capable to me."

She couldn't help letting her gaze move down his chest. He looked way more than capable, if she were being totally honest. He'd stayed in his workout clothes as had she when they got back to his place, and she'd had a hard time keeping her eyes off his muscular arms and legs.

"Oh, I'm more than capable," he said. "There's only one thing I have to know before we take this any further."

"Sure," she said.

This? What did he mean, *this*? Was he talking about the bill or their affair? She kept cool. One of the things she was good as was keeping her emotions in check when she needed to and this definitely seemed like a good time to do that. Except she wasn't cool. But her silly heart was racing a bit and she realized she wanted to be able to give him whatever it was he wanted from her.

What if…it danced through her mind and she

knew she was tempted to make this affair into something else.

Why?

What did her psyche sense that her rational mind was missing?

"Will you be ethical about the promises you make while you lobby the other senators to keep them from voting for my bill?" he asked.

"Always. Listen, I've apologized for the way I misled you when we met, but I wanted a chance to get to know the man behind the headlines and I took a gamble. There was a chance you could have thrown me out or that I would never have met you, but that didn't happen. Going forward I won't be lying again."

And she meant it. She hadn't liked lying to him or the way she felt when he'd found her out. She wasn't going to put herself in that situation again. Not with him or anybody else.

"I'm glad you took the gamble," he said, leaning closer to her. "I'm very glad we met."

She nodded, then reached out to push a curl that had fallen onto his forehead back. He caught her hand in his and brought it to his mouth, kissing her palm, and she realized that she was going to take that what-if path. She was going to do this and see where it led.

For the first time in her life she was going to do something for herself and not because it forwarded her career.

Eight

Her fingers against his skin were soft and cool. He held his breath as her hands moved down his jaw. He wanted her. That was it. He'd been trying to be calm and keep his wits about him, but this was Melody and for some reason thinking wasn't part of the equation when she was around. He knew this, and it would have been sensible to get up and call it a night, but instead he scooped her off her chair and over onto his lap.

"So…?"

She was never going to give anything to him easily, he thought. She kept him guessing every moment he was with her. And he knew that was a big part of her appeal, yet at the same time, he wanted to believe he could move on. That this temporary sexual thing that was happening between the two of them would consume them for a few short weeks and then they'd both go their separate ways. He'd either get the votes he needed for the bill he'd spent his entire Senate career working on or she'd help her team defeat him.

And that was life in DC.

What happened tonight truly had nothing to do with it. He didn't kid himself that he could change her mind or influence her in any way that would make her stop working against him.

"So, I thought you looked uncomfortable over there," he said.

"I thought *you* looked uncomfortable," she countered.

"Did you? In what way?"

"Like your shirt was too hot. I mean, it is summer. Sure, the evening is a bit cooler but the heat from the day is still in the air," she said.

He felt his erection stir and he was sure she noticed it, too, as her left thigh was right on top of it. He just nodded his head as if he were contemplating her comment. "I am hot, but it can sometimes come off as rude to whip my shirt off in front of a lady."

"Yeah, I can see how some women might be offended. But I never would," she said, shifting back and taking the hem of his T-shirt in her hand. "Want some help getting it off?"

Hell, yeah. "Sure, if you don't mind."

She took her time, slowly raising his shirt and stopping when his abs were bare. She ran her fingers along his ribs, tickling him and making him laugh. She arched both eyebrows looking up at him. "I like your laugh."

So fascinating. She was going to be the death of him if he couldn't figure her out. "Thanks. Are you ticklish?"

"You'll have to find out," she said.

He tugged her shirt up and over her head, putting it on the chair she'd been sitting in so Bailey didn't sniff it or try to eat it. Then he ran his finger along the line where the elastic from her sports bra met her skin. She shivered but didn't laugh. "Not ticklish here."

"I guess you'll have to keep trying to find a spot."

"Probably. I'm a thorough man," he said.

"I like that about you," she replied.

"What else do you like?" he asked, leaning closer so that his lips brushed hers as he spoke.

But her mouth was too tempting, and he couldn't help kissing her. She tasted better than he remembered, and he didn't know how that was possible. Should that be a red flag?

Who the hell cared?

Her hand moved lower on his stomach and her finger circled his belly button, which made him even harder. He thrust his tongue deep into her mouth and she responded by angling her head to the side to deepen their embrace.

He held her with one hand against her back, his finger stroking in a small circle in the center, and she arched her shoulders, which pushed her breasts against his chest. He let his fingers sprawl on her warm skin and held her against him. She put her hands on his face and looked into his eyes. Her brown eyes were liquid pools of chocolate that he wanted to lose himself in.

"I like too much about you," she said, then kissed him again before he had time to think about what she'd said.

Damn.

The woman knew how to kiss. And for a man who prided himself on being rational, he wasn't as bothered as he should be by the fact that when she was in his arms all he wanted was to make love to her.

He wanted to blame this obsession on how they'd met and the fact that she'd had an ulterior motive. But he knew that wasn't the reason he was fixated on her.

He liked her.

And there hadn't been that many women he'd felt this way about in the course of his life. He'd slept with only two of them because a smart man who liked living his life on his own terms didn't sleep with someone who could tie him down.

He pulled his head back and looked down at her. Trying to see if she was using him. Trying to remind himself that this time he was going to use her. Trying to find the willpower to stop this before it went any further.

But he couldn't say no to her.

Instead he lifted her into his arms and carried her

inside his town house and up the stairs to his bedroom. He walked past the pictures of his family on the wall and saw his father grinning out at him from one of them. Dare paused for a moment.

This was his legacy. Taking the wrong woman to bed and not giving a damn about the consequences.

Was he okay with that?

"Dare?" Melody asked, putting her hand on his face again. Those long fingers against his jaw made him realize that he was definitely okay.

He wasn't willing to let her go. Not tonight at least.

She hadn't planned on sleeping with him tonight, but she had the feeling that with Dare she'd better take things as they came. She had no idea what was in his head or his heart, but for herself she wanted this affair. She wanted to experience something… no, not something vague, she wanted to experience *him*. Wanted to give herself the chance to be with this man who made her senses come alive in a way they never really had before.

He was staring at a family portrait that hung on his wall and Melody couldn't help but look at it as well. The Bisset family had that all-American preppy, rich vibe that she'd never really paid much attention to. Her family had never been poor and she hadn't wanted for anything, but as she looked at the Bissets all standing together in front of a huge house on the beach, she started to get the feeling that there was a lot more to Dare than just being a senator or the eldest son. When she saw that photo, she couldn't help but think of his legacy.

She imagined he must think about that often.

"Dare?" she repeated.

Had he changed his mind about sleeping with her? The enemy. The person who was determined to do whatever she could to keep his bill from passing? She would completely get it if he had.

"Yeah," he said. "Sorry. It's just that sometimes the harder I try to distance myself from one path the more that fate seems to shove me back onto it."

"Put me down," she said. This wasn't just him debating about sleeping with her; this was Dare at the crossroads of something bigger, and she had no clue as to what. To be honest, this might be more than she'd bargained for. He set her on her feet.

Hot sex with someone who was definitely forbidden to her was one thing. But his sudden seriousness was complicating things. She wanted the fun, flirty guy who'd teased her into taking off her shirt earlier. Not this brooding man. Of course, she liked the brooding bit sometimes, but she realized it was different when she cared about the man.

And she'd already realized earlier that she did care for him. That there was more here than a sexy spark that made her want to take risks.

This was another layer of that risk. Was she daring enough to just go for it? To take what she needed from him, knowing that she'd never be objective where he was concerned after this night? Actually, was she even objective now?

Hell.

Why hadn't anyone warned her that sex could have these kinds of complications? That it could be about something more than having fun and feeling good?

She looked at him again. Those bright blue eyes and that thick black hair that fell rakishly over his forehead. Damn. She wasn't going to be smart and leave. She just wasn't. She'd pretty much decided that wherever this went she was in it until they crashed out.

She knew that there was no happily-ever-after for them and she was okay with that. Dare was older, his career established. He was also fascinating, and despite this conversation, she was still turned on. That was all she needed to know. Something about him drew her and she wasn't willing to let it be.

"What path do you want to be on?" she asked at last.

He shook his head. "One with you."

She thought he was deflecting with that answer. "Don't be cute. Or do be cute but then don't be serious. You turn me on by flirting with me and making me stop thinking about the complications and then you get here and say leading things that make me want to know more and then cut me off. What is it you want? I know I played you at the reception, but I thought we'd moved past that."

He shoved his hand into his hair and turned away from her, cursing under his breath. When he turned, she noticed the long, jagged scar on his right shoulder that she hadn't noticed when they'd slept together. She reached out and touched it. Ran her finger down the length of it. It wasn't rough, so she assumed it was old.

He glanced back over his shoulder at her and then reached for her hand and drew her around and into his arms. "I want more than I have a right to ask you for. And I think we both know that this is a bad idea, but at the same time it feels right."

She smiled at the truth in his words because it echoed what was in her mind, too. "I know. There's no future and we have the past. Let's just be and enjoy it. I'm not looking at your family and thinking someday I'm going to be next to you in a group photo. I know that we are just this hot summer fling."

"I just don't want to end up being someone you regret," he said.

His words stopped her. What did he know that she didn't? Was it just age and experience talking? Did he have an ulterior motive?

"I don't want that, either. So let's both promise to be good to each other and no more sneakiness," she said. "That's my promise to you."

He looked into her eyes and she felt something pass between them, but it was complicated and not something she was comfortable admitting she felt. So she closed her eyes and when she opened them, he nodded. "How about I drive you home?"

"Changed your mind about finding my tickle spot?"

"Oh, no. Not me. I'm going to run my hands all over your body until I do find it," he said. "But are you still in the mood for that?"

Hell, yes. He'd just put in her head the image of her naked and him touching her. Her heart started to beat a little faster and she felt empty and aching between her legs. She wanted him. She wanted a night with him where she didn't have to worry about anything other than pleasing him.

"Oh, yes."

Dare had had enough of talking and not taking. He had invited her to join him tonight because he wanted her. Wanted to have her, knowing exactly who she was, and he was tired of getting in his own way. Melody was here and he didn't want to waste a minute of the time they had left.

He took her hand in his, spreading his fingers until he could link their hands together. He looked down at her long fingers with her short but polished nails and smiled. Those short nails made her real. She didn't have a gel manicure to make her seem more polished and he liked it. It was just one of the ways that she was inconsistent and yet so Melody.

The more time he spent with her the more he appreciated the humor and honesty that were so much a part of who she was.

He tugged her hand and she came forward until their chests were touching. He felt the exhalation of her breath against his chest. He looked down at her blond hair and stopped thinking. She tipped her head back and arched one eyebrow up at him. Then she ran the fingers of her free hand along his rib cage, making him laugh and pull back from her. He lifted her off her feet and hefted her over his shoulder in a fireman's carry, taking her into his bedroom. She continued tickling him and as soon as was close enough to the king-size bed, he carefully dropped her on it. She bounced and then propped herself up on her elbows to watch him.

He stood there looking at the navy comforter and realized his bed was never going to be the same again. He was always going to picture her grinning and tempting him on it. He turned quickly, went into the bathroom and opened the medicine cabinet to get out a condom before returning. While he was gone, she'd taken off her sports bra and running shorts and shoes and was totally naked. Just lying there on her side waiting for him.

He skimmed his gaze over her body, lingering on her breasts, the curve of her hip and the tempting feminine flesh at the apex of her thighs. The neatly trimmed dark blond hair that concealed her secrets.

"Looks like someone is falling behind," she teased.

He toed off his shoes and socks, then pushed his running shorts and underwear down his legs and stepped out of them. He ripped open the foil packet and put the condom on before he moved to the bed.

He put his knee on it and nudged her shoulder

gently until she rolled onto her back. He straddled her and then sat back on his haunches, looking down at her spread out underneath him.

Her skin was pale and her nipples a reddish pink that seemed to darken as they tightened. He reached down, rubbing them with his thumbs and letting his fingers slide down her sides until he could push one hand under her back, arching her toward him.

He leaned down, sucking the tip of her nipple into his mouth as he let his other hand roam her body. He didn't think about anything other than how she felt so smooth and soft under his touch.

Her hands were in his hair, one of them keeping his head at her breast while the other roamed down his stomach, her finger circling his belly button and making him even harder before she moved lower. He felt the brush of her touch against his shaft before she cupped his balls. She bit the lobe of his ear at the same time and his hips jerked forward, his erection rubbing against her belly.

He lifted his head from her breast, watching her eyes close as he continued to caress her. He loved the way she felt under his hands and wanted more. He shifted lower to lick at her clit until her hips were moving frantically under him, and when she grabbed his shoulders, calling out his name as her thighs closed around his head, he suspected she'd come.

He moved up her body, bracing his hands on either side of her shoulders, pushing one of them into her hair. He found the opening of her body with the tip of his erection and thrust deeply into her.

He brought his mouth down on hers, closing his eyes as he drove himself into her again and again. He felt shivering down his spine and his balls tightened as she dug her nails into his back, arching against him and calling his name as he felt her tighten around him. He kept driving into her until he came with a loud grunt.

He thrust until he felt emptied all the way to his soul and then collapsed on top of her, careful to support his weight with his knees and his hands to keep from crushing her.

She languidly stroked his back as their breathing slowed to normal and he rolled to his side, cuddling her against him. She had her head on his shoulder, and kept caressing him, He held her, hoping that she'd let this moment last. Because he knew if he started talking to her, he was going to have to make a decision about whether or not he could continue to lie to himself and say this was just a summer fling.

She got to him like no woman had in a very long time and that worried him. Because the last time he'd felt this way, his life had imploded, and he'd been left trying to pick up pieces that no longer fit together.

Nine

Melody showered and dressed in the sweats that Dare had loaned her. She had already called an Uber to go home. Dare had offered to drive her but honestly how awkward would it be if anyone saw her getting out of his car?

She wasn't prepared to deal with that. Not tonight and not tomorrow, either, she admitted to herself. She used the towel to dry her hair and then left the master bathroom after having a sniff of Dare's aftershave. A part of her wanted to pretend that once she left his house everything was going to go back to her version of normal.

But even she had a hard time swallowing that lie. She knew that her life was going to be different.

And she'd wanted that.

She had been tired of always being the same Melody. This change was one she'd craved for a while now and she welcomed it. She was taking a personal risk, which she'd never done before. She'd always focused hard on the job, on winning, but this was something else. Dare was making her look at herself and her life with different eyes. And she had to admit it was exciting.

She wasn't sure if it was exciting because she'd never done anything like this before or if it was something in Dare.

When she came back into the master bedroom, she noticed that Dare had put her sweaty gym clothes into a duffel bag embroidered with Moretti Racing logo on the side. She picked it up before heading downstairs and found him on the patio with Bailey, tossing a chewed-up tennis ball to the dog, who retrieved it and then waited for Dare to throw it again.

She just watched him being a normal dude for a few more seconds before she shook her head. She was too smart to fall for Dare Bisset. Senator Darien Bisset, who was on the opposite side of the issues from her. Who was in a different world than she was.

She repeated those sentences in her head like a litany, hoping that the message would stick but there was a part of her that wasn't listening. And she knew it.

She could tell because when he turned and waved at her, she smiled and waved back. Then she stood there for a minute just smiling at him before she realized that she needed to snap out of it.

She was definitely going to call her brother as soon as she got home and let him talk some sense into her. Help her readjust and get back on track. But until then…

"Hello. I see you found the bag I put your stuff in," he said.

"Thanks. Why do you have a Moretti Racing bag? Are you a fan of Formula One?"

"I'm not a fan. My sister's fiancé is a driver. Inigo Velasquez," he said. "Not sure if you're a fan."

"I'm not but my dad is. Wow, this is the second person who's related to you that my family would completely lose their shit over," she said, then realized how silly that might sound. But the words finally started to penetrate the sunny haze she'd been allowing herself to mellow in since she'd gotten here.

Dare wasn't just a little bit different from her. He existed in a world that she had no part in. A world where she was the screaming fan girl and he was the mega star. Oh, damn.

Shit.

That was exactly what she was. She was here because he was a rock star on Capitol Hill. The kind of senator everyone liked and sort of feared because they knew he'd find a way to get his bills through. And she was trying to take him down?

How did she even—

"Well, Inigo is just a regular guy," Dare said, interrupting her thoughts. "He's just wicked good at driving. And you saw that Toby was a normal dad."

"Yeah," she agreed. But sure it was easy for Dare to say someone was just a regular person when his social circle including presidents, celebrities, a billionaire father and the paparazzi. That would never feel normal to her.

"What is it? I'm not like that. I live in this place that's pretty middle of the road," he said. "Not fancy. Not jet-setting like Inigo or Toby."

But he was fancy. She knew he downplayed it. Not just right now to her, he downplayed it for the voters. He wanted to appear to be the common man and she had almost fallen for that. Had almost let herself believe it when she'd first come here. When she'd watched him giving Bailey ice cream after a job on a hot summer's evening. But he was still the man in that family photograph upstairs.

American royalty.

And there was no way around it. She was middle class. She might have a white-collar job working for a powerful lobbyist in Washington but at the end of the day…she wasn't in Dare's league.

And that seemed bigger and more of a hurdle than the fact that they were rivals.

"Mel, you okay?"

She nodded even though she wasn't. No one called her Mel. She'd just never been the type of woman anyone called by a nickname, but she liked it when he did it.

Well, enjoy it for now, she told herself. Starting

tomorrow she was going to be all business. This ended here.

"Yeah. I just think I was fooling myself and you to some extent when I thought we could do this and not have to face any consequences. I don't think this is going to work."

"It will…it can. Just give it a chance," he said. "Give me a chance. I like you. I wish that you were just some random woman I met at my cousin's wedding. Then this would work, wouldn't it?"

She doubted it. Because it wasn't the work thing that worried her the most. It was his lifestyle and the fact that she'd feel like a hanger-on. Despite the fact that he'd never want her to think of herself that way, she knew how it would look. There was an age gap between them. She was from a middle-class family. It looked like she was reaching for something.

She looked up and saw Dare watching her. Saw the expression on his face and she wanted to just say yes to anything he proposed because she liked him. She wanted to please him. But was that the smart thing to do? Or just one more mistake?

Dare worked out in the gym in his town house complex and then got to his office by seven. A lot of senators took their time getting in but he had scheduled a staff meeting to get the ball rolling on countering any of the momentum that Johnny Rosemond and his team had on opposing his bill. He knew they had a lot of money in their pocket and as Melody had alluded to, a lot of the pharmaceutical companies did offer rebates to consumers but for many that still didn't help make the drugs affordable.

Cami was there before him, directing two interns in setting up the conference room they used and making sure they had an assortment of healthy breakfast options and hot beverages. He left her to it and went into his office, remembering his conversation with Logan the night before as it helped him to not think about Melody. He sent a text to Nick's father to see if he had time for a call later. He also texted Adler, not wanting to interrupt her honeymoon but needing to make sure his cousin and Nick weren't blindsided by the business controversy Logan had stirred up when they got back. Dare didn't expect a response from her right away, so he started answering emails.

He had one from his father that was directly related to the bill he was trying to pass. Since it would place limits on Bisset Industries' pharmaceutical division, Dare wasn't surprised that his father wanted to meet for drinks later in the week to "discuss" options. That was August Bisset speak for giving ultimatums to his children. Even though Dare was well over thirty, his father still acted like a good talking-to would change Dare's mind. He emailed back telling him he'd meet with him because it was easier to deal with his father on his terms.

There was a knock on the frame of his open office door. He glanced up to see Cami standing there. "Everything's almost set up."

"Good. Was there something else you needed?" he asked but that information hadn't warranted an office visit.

"Yes…maybe. Listen, that staffer on Rosemond's team, the young girl. She called after you left and asked where you'd be running. I was vague and mentioned you ran with Bailey, but it almost sounded like she'd been stalking you."

Oh, dear God. This wasn't what he expected. "She wasn't stalking me. I think I made things awkward by waving when I ran by her. She probably called to make sure it was me."

"Oh," Cami said. "Glad you cleared that up."

"Yeah, well, was there anything else?" he asked her. He wasn't going to discuss this any further with his assistant.

"Not this morning."

"Good. I forwarded you a calendar request from my dad. Can you book us some place for drinks and possibly dinner on Wednesday or Thursday?"

"Sure. Anything else?"

"I'm expecting a personal call sometime this morning, so if I get it, I might have to leave our strategy session for a few minutes. I'll need you to take over."

"Sure thing," she said. "The team takes direction better from me anyway."

"If you say so," he responded.

They went into the strategy meeting and Dare got them started with the number of senators they'd need on their side before he could take his bill to the floor. The issues involved were complex and lobbyists were working both sides of the aisle hard, so the voting would probably not be down party lines. The challenge was one that he was looking forward to. Dare knew he was going to have to work hard to get the votes he needed.

His staff was small but eager and as they mapped out their strategy, Dare couldn't help but wonder if Melody was in a similar meeting working hard for Johnny to try to stop his bill. He knew she was. Why was he even thinking of her?

"Dare."

"Hmm?"

"Your phone," Cami said, pointing at it.

It was Adler. "Thanks. I'll be right back."

He answered the call as soon as he'd stepped out of the conference room.

"Hey, cuz. I know you wouldn't bother me unless this was important but I'm almost afraid to ask what's up," Adler said.

"Sorry, Ad. I actually need to talk to Nick, too. Is he there?" Dare asked.

"Yes. Hold on, let me put you on speaker," she said.

"Hey, Dare, it's Nick."

Dare took a deep breath. Honestly, he'd rather be calling recalcitrant senators than making this call. "Um, I talked to Logan last night and wanted to give you a heads-up. Apparently, Logan deliberately bought a patent that Williams International needed just to undercut Nick's business?"

"He was being an ass. He was angry that I was marrying Adler and he took our rivalry a step too far. But we cleared that up in Nantucket," Nick said. "He's going to sell me the patent."

"I don't know. He called me last night and said the deal has hit a snag. Part of the problem is that it leaked to the press and there have been some negative stories freaking both of our families out," Dare said. "I know it's your honeymoon, but I wanted to give you a heads-up in case you see any of these stories. Logan is still trying to fix things—he hasn't changed his mind about wanting to reconcile."

"Why would he do this? And Nick, why didn't you tell me about this earlier?" Adler asked. Dare could hear the anger and frustration in her voice.

"Logan felt cornered and he hates to lose in the competition between us. But since we found out we're brothers, we're trying to move past that. Adler, I didn't want to add to the stress you were already feeling over the scandal at our wedding."

Adler was silent, so Dare jumped in.

"Nick, is it possible to set up a call or something so that we can get this resolved once and for all?" he asked. "I've also reached out to your father, who's very upset about the news stories."

"Yeah. I'll get your number from Adler and text you. I assume you'll help smooth things over? I actually don't want my father involved in this."

"You're right. And I'm happy to help, and be a line of communication between you and Logan. I don't want our fathers involved, either. But I'll speak to them to calm them down," Dare said.

"Okay. I'll get back to you later," Nick said.

"I'll keep my phone with me. I have two meetings that I won't be able to break out of immediately but will get back to you as soon as possible after."

"Fair enough."

"Sorry to bring bad news but I didn't want you two to have another surprise after everything you've dealt with," Dare said.

"Thanks, Dare. I know it's not your fault, but I really don't like my Bisset relatives right now," Adler said.

"I don't blame you."

It was after nine before Melody was done for the day and headed home. Her brother had texted to say he could chat, so she was looking forward to him giving her the kind of hard-hitting advice that she'd never really needed before. But something about Dare had knocked her off her axis.

It had been nice to be so busy at work that she didn't have time to really obsess over him. Of course, it hadn't helped that one of her assignments had been to compile a dossier on Dare and his associates. But she'd done it. When she started breaking down the facts on the other senators who were also putting the bill forward it had been way too easy to see the ways that Dare was different.

The ways that Dare was better, in her opinion. But she kept that to herself and just did her work. She was on a team with seasoned lobbyists, some of whom had been instrumental in shaping legislation for the last twenty years, and she didn't want to make herself seem even more junior by going gaga over Dare. So she'd kept it to herself. Made notes and calls and booked dinners for Johnny to go and schmooze prospective allies among the senators.

Being in the thick of things had reminded her of how much she loved her job. She hadn't been sure if this was the right career choice. She'd had a paid internship at a law firm before she graduated and that hadn't suited her. Her father had hoped either she or her brother would do corporate law for the job security, but it didn't excite her the way that this did.

She could easily see herself working as a lobbyist for the rest of her career. So she really had to take stock of this thing with Dare and be careful.

She was risking throwing away a meaningful, fulfilling career. And she didn't kid herself that she'd be able to keep working in this field if it ever got out that she had an affair with Dare.

When she got home, she microwaved a packet of rice, dumped it in a bowl and doused it with soy sauce. Then she opened up her laptop and ate at her breakfast bar while working and waiting for her brother to video chat with her.

When the call came in, she answered it quickly and smiled at her brother. He was a junior defense attorney working for a big criminal law firm in Boston.

"Hey. I was going to apologize for not being able to talk sooner but you are still eating dinner…long day?"

"Yeah," she said. "But it was a good long day, you know?"

"I do. I never thought I'd hear you say that," he admitted. "You hated working long hours at the firm."

"I did hate it. It just wasn't for me. This is more my thing," she said. "And because of that… I need you to be real with me, Ben."

"When haven't I been?"

"Well, that one time when I thought I should do the final argument in that debate—" she said, remembering in high school when he'd sided with her even though another debate team member's argument was stronger.

"I'm your big brother. Of course I was going to side with you," he said.

"I know. But this time don't."

"You're starting to worry me," he said.

She swallowed and then nodded. "I may have slept with Dare Bisset."

"Okay. He's a senator…wasn't he at that wedding you crashed?"

"Yes. He's the senator whose bill we are trying to defeat," she said. "I went to meet him to get intel and then things happened."

"You're… I want to have your back but this is serious. Was it just at the wedding? If so, that should be fine. One night isn't a big thing," Ben said. "You're worrying about nothing. Just relax and enjoy doing a job you like."

She sighed. "I slept with him again last night."

"Oh. Okay, so is this a thing? Now, you're worrying me. Do you actually like him?" Ben asked.

She wasn't sure. Which was a total lie. She liked him. "I do like him. I mean I know I shouldn't, and I cannot keep seeing him. Tell me that."

Ben started laughing and reached for a Red Bull and took a swallow. "If you are asking me to tell you, then you already know. I think you want to run through what will happen if you keep seeing him."

"What will happen?" she asked, realizing she did need her brother's counsel on this. Ben understood her better than she did sometimes.

"Okay, so assuming neither of you is going to get ticked when the other wins on the Senate floor, which we know won't be true on your side," Ben started, "then we have to consider if anyone else will be affected by your relationship."

"I'm not going to be ticked. I won't be happy but as long as I do the best I can and it's a fair fight I'm okay," she said.

"I think you found your answer, Mel. I can't tell you what to do, you know that. But I think you've already thought about this too much."

She nodded. She had done nothing but think about Dare and the entire situation in every spare second she had. She wanted to say it was just sex. Or the excitement of the forbidden affair. But she knew it was something deeper.

"His family is ridiculously wealthy. We really don't have anything in common."

"It sounds like you do," he said.

"Why aren't you helping?"

"I am helping you with the truth. You've never talked about a guy before and I have to think if you are now, then this one is different. His wealth doesn't matter if he's a good man. If he's a decent guy, then you have nothing to worry about."

"I wish I could believe that," she said quietly.

"When you do then you'll have your answer," he said. "Are you going to be home anytime soon?"

"Not sure. Why?"

"Mom is pressuring me to come home and I smell a setup."

She laughed. "You're mom's favorite so if you tell her you don't want her setting you up, she'll stop."

He didn't say anything and she shook her head. "You want her to, don't you."

"Maybe. I mean, Mom knows me better than anyone and my track record hasn't been great," he said. "Did you ever consider you and I aren't great at love?"

"All the time," she said.

She ended the call with her brother a few minutes later and went to sleep with Ben's words on her mind. Was Dare a decent man?

Ten

The week hadn't been what Dare would call productive. Especially given that Johnny Rosemond's star player—Melody—had been beating his team to the punch, swaying a number of key senators on this bill. He knew it wasn't personal. The issue of fixed prescription pricing was a thorny one that Congress hadn't resolved despite decades of trying. It was a cutthroat battle and both sides fought to win.

And Dare sort of got it. He came from a family that had been making money for generations off the backs of regular workers. But he wanted to change all of that. He had a few witnesses lined up to testify before the committee about their situations that he knew would turn the tide. Only someone who was heartless would vote against a single mom with a child with a chronic illness and poor prescription coverage.

But first he had his father to deal with. He was having drinks and dinner with him tonight, and Dare wasn't looking forward to fending off his questions about the bill and how it would affect Bisset Industries. And of course there was the issue with Nick and Logan that Dare still had to take care of.

His father was waiting at one of the high tables in the back of the bar. He waved Dare over when he arrived, but Dare stopped by the bar to order a martini first, as he knew that was his father's favorite drink.

"Hello, Dad. How's things?" he asked as he sat down across from his father. Dare knew that some families were all huggy but his father never had been. His mom would have given him a kiss on the cheek but his dad didn't do that kind of touchy-feely stuff.

"They're going. About what you'd expect at home. And Logan is shutting me out at work. Now that he's the CEO I guess I have to respect that," August said. He finished off his martini and signaled the waitress for another one.

"I'm sorry," Dare said.

His father gave a dry laugh. "I'm sure you are."

"Dad, despite our differences I always thought your life worked for you. So I'm sorry it's been so rough lately."

"Thanks, son. Gran always warned me about not realizing what I had until it was gone and I guess she was right."

Dare wasn't sure what his father was getting at. Damn. Were his parents divorcing? Was that what this private one-on-one was about? Dare had always been the buffer between his siblings and his parents. But he wasn't ready to bring this kind of news back to his brothers and sister.

"What's going on? Is mom leaving you?" he asked. He might be able to be suave and subtle when it came to dealing with legislation but when it came to his family he always lost that cool reserve.

"Not yet," he said. "I don't know. We're not living together. She went back to the Hamptons and suggested that I'd be happier in the city. So I've been staying there."

"Is that what you wanted?" Dare asked.

"No. Definitely not. But I can't… I hurt your mom deeply, Dare. I can't stand seeing that pain on her face. And she feels guilty about Logan, which I know is still my fault," August said.

"I get it. I know you're used to kind of blustering and then letting things blow over, but this time you might have to go and talk to her. Tell her how you really feel," Dare said as a blonde woman caught his eye at the bar. She reminded him of Melody with her long hair falling to her shoulders and the slim cut of her summer dress hugging her curves.

She turned.

It was Melody.

He almost went over to say hello but she rushed to greet another man. Hell. She was meeting with Tad

Williams. Why? His company didn't have a stake in pharmaceuticals. What was she playing at? Was she meeting with Tad—

"Dare?"

He turned his attention back to his father. "Sorry. I just saw someone I know."

"Who?" his father asked.

"The woman with Tad," Dare said.

"She was at the wedding with you, wasn't she?" August asked. "Why is she meeting with Williams?"

His father said the surname like it was a curse and Dare had to agree in this moment.

"I don't know. She's working with Johnny Rosemond to stop my bill from being passed. I can't imagine Tad has a stake in controlling prescription costs or regulating big pharma."

Dare braced himself for a tirade from his father about the bill but it didn't come. Instead August focused his diatribe on Tad.

"He doesn't have a stake in pharmaceuticals. But anytime you talk of defunding any big business everyone gets jumpy. And he doesn't like our family... especially now that he knows I'm the biological father of his eldest son."

Of course being a Bisset would come between him and Melody. He didn't know what to make of her meeting with Tad. He had the same feeling as when she'd walked into his office with Johnny's team. She was wily and he could appreciate her ambition; it was one of the things that drew him to her, albeit reluctantly. But given the way he felt about her, it made his life more complicated than he wanted it to be.

"What is the deal between you two?" Dare asked after a pause in the conversation. "Seems like it's more than just a business rivalry." His father rubbed the back of his neck and shook his head. "Tad used to work for Bisset Industries. He was in love with Aunt Kelly and the family didn't approve, so we put an end to the relationship and had Tad fired from the company."

"The family or you?"

"Me. He wasn't from the right sort of family. It felt to me that he saw Aunt Kelly as an easy way to get what he wanted from life. So I did what I had to do. I wasn't going to allow my sister to be used."

Dare could appreciate that as he would do anything to protect Mari, but he suspected his father had done more than put his sister's interest first. "And he hates you because you tried to ruin him. I guess he proved you wrong about not being successful. He worked hard to make Williams, Inc., into what it is today. He didn't take the easy route."

"Yes, he did. Turns out I was wrong about a lot of things," August said. "Learn from mistakes, son. Don't let jealousy and ambition keep you from the good things in life."

He glanced over at Melody and their eyes met and something passed between them. Lust he could handle. But was there something more? Was she a good thing?

* * *

Of course Dare would be meeting his father at the same bar and restaurant that Tad Williams had picked for their meeting. It was a bit daunting to see her lover and his father while she was meeting with the man who was their rival and enemy.

She hadn't been sleeping well since she'd spoken to her brother, and had been working long hours. But she had still found time to read up on the drama between the Bissets and the Williamses and had learned that it had been going on for the better part of the last forty years.

When Tad had reached out to Johnny, offering to put him in touch with some power players who could help block Dare's bill, Johnny had assigned the meeting to her. Many on the team, herself included, felt that Tad was reaching out simply because of the rivalry between his family and Dare's. No one thought he could bring anything new to the table.

So here she was doing the grunt work. And of course Dare was here.

She knew how this would look. She felt cringey about it herself, knowing they'd slept together. Knowing that she'd been duplicitous the moment they met. This was going to be another mark against her in their personal life.

Maybe that was a good thing. Maybe this would be the kick she needed to stop pining over him. To get her drive and ambition back so that she would stop worrying about his feelings and just do what she could to block his bill.

Except she knew the bill and Dare were two completely different things to her. Still, there was that gray area in between business and pleasure with Dare, and she couldn't help staying in it.

"Thanks for taking this meeting," Tad said, shaking her hand.

She noticed that he had an easy smile and laugh lines around his eyes. His hair was salt-and-pepper but still full and his eyes a brilliant blue color.

"It's my pleasure," she said. "I know you'd hoped to talk to Johnny, but as I'm the newest on the team my calendar is the lightest. I hope you don't mind."

"Not at all. I started my career the same way," Tad said. "What can I get you to drink?"

She'd been warned by both of her parents to be careful about drinking while on the job. So she just ordered a soda water with a twist of lime even though the summer cocktail—a watermelon martini—sounded delicious.

"I think you have to place your first order at the bar and then the waitresses will bring refills. Do you want to find a table while I get our drinks?" he suggested.

"Sounds good," she said, looking for an empty table and spotting one near the back. She made a beeline for it, not wanting to lose it in the crowded bar. She kept her gaze fixated on her destination as she walked right past Dare and his father.

The closer she got the more she tried not to glance at Dare, but she couldn't help it; she looked up just as she passed him.

She smiled at him. She couldn't help it.

He just arched one eyebrow at her and she realized he did see this as a betrayal as she'd suspected he would. Fair enough. She was meeting with a man who hated him and his family. She got it.

She turned away from him and when she got to the empty high table, she took a seat so that her back was to Dare. She didn't want to see him again.

She tried to remind herself that this was what she knew needed to happen. That a clean break between them would be the only solution to her ridiculous feelings. She wasn't a woman given to emotion before, so why should the situation with Dare be any different?

She pulled her phone from her bag and scrolled through her email, trying to distract herself and get back into meeting mode. She had a feeling that Tad hadn't reached out just to stump Dare. He struck her as a man with purpose and she was going to make the most of the meeting. And if Dare Bisset thought she was doing this just to screw him up…well, so be it.

She had her whole career in front of her and a life of her own to build. One that he wouldn't play any enduring part in.

"Here you go," Tad said, sitting down across from her and placing the drinks on the table.

"Thank you. So, you know what project we are

working on and it might be awkward to talk about it with the senator overseeing the committee sitting right over there."

"I do," he said. "I'm okay with it if you are. He knows that I won't be putting my money or support behind a bill that threatens business on the scale that he is proposing."

"He's mainly going after big pharma," she said. But she knew the language in his bill left room for other industries that took government grants to be targeted down the road.

"Yes, but we both know that's not all he's after. I guess if August Bisset was my father, I'd want to dismantle big business as well, just to spite him. I'm surprised to see them together. They have always been at each other's throats."

She wasn't sure that Tad should be talking about Dare's personal life, but she definitely got that he and August hated each other. It was there in how he spoke about the other man. Something that underlined his tone.

"What is it exactly that you wanted to discuss with me?" she asked, turning the subject back to business. "I don't want to talk about the senator's personal details."

"Of course not. A lot of the senators' staffs have brought up that they don't want to nix the bill entirely. Their constituencies are concerned about drug pricing and development. I have reached out and I may have something else that will be useful to you.

I understand that testimonials from ordinary people are important to demonstrating why big pharma should be regulated, but I think I can help you come up with stories about how big pharma has helped the lives of regular men and women. My wife volunteers at a women's shelter in Boston and she works with two clients there who would be hurt by government defunding pharmaceutical research, which I understand is part of the bill. I thought it might help you to hear from them. To show that there is more to this issue than just cheap drugs for everyone."

She nodded and took notes. She spent the next forty-five minutes pretending that she didn't know that Dare was behind her, and it didn't help when he got up to leave that she immediately felt his loss.

She was beginning to think that maybe this wasn't the right path for her. She had believed she could do her job as a lobbyist and have an affair with him, but had she been fooling herself?

Dare told himself that he was just waiting to see how long her meeting lasted. He knew that was a lie but his father's hotel was across the street from the bar and when his father invited him to join him for dinner in the outdoor seating area there, Dare agreed. He told himself he wasn't waiting for her for any reason other than business.

But that lie didn't work. His father was in a talkative mood; in fact, it was the first time that Dare could remember that he was actually enjoying hanging out with his father. Maybe it was age taking the edge off the relationship or his father's recent bout of humility but Dare didn't question it.

"I'm thinking about buying your mother a villa in Italy. She always wanted one and it could be a big gesture that will show her I truly regret what happened."

Dare laughed as he listened to his father trying to justify buying a villa for his mom. "Dad, that's not the kind of big gesture I meant. Though I wouldn't mind if we had an Italian villa in the family. But when you extend an olive branch, it should be a gesture that means something to just the two of you."

"What would you get Melody?" his father asked.

"Nothing. We're not married, and I haven't screwed up," Dare said.

"Are you sure? When she walked by the table—"

"Don't. I am not talking about her with you," Dare said. Hell, he wasn't talking about her with anyone. Everything between the two of them was over. He had a feeling that having a secret affair was a bad idea, but he'd wanted…it no longer mattered. She was here in DC for her career, not for him. And there was no gesture he could make that would change that.

"I get that. But if you want some advice from someone who's been there and screwed up, then if she means something to you, don't put her last," August said. "Believe me, you'll regret it and eventually it will start to eat at you."

He was surprised to hear his father admit to regretting anything. "Really?"

"Yes. If you'd told me when I was thirty-five that I'd feel this way, I would have thought it was ridiculous. But when I look back at all the important things that I put ahead of your mom and the rest of you, they don't seem that important now," he said. "I think you can see how I've managed to keep screwing up with family and at one time I could almost justify it by looking at the bottom line, but those days are gone. Someday you're not going to be working twenty-four seven and trying to outmaneuver everyone else and if you're at all like me—and you are—you'll realize that you've maneuvered yourself into a lonely existence."

Dare stared at his father and then reached over and put his hand on top of his dad's and squeezed it. He'd always known August Bisset was a smart man, but this was the first time when anything he said had resonated so deeply with Dare. He'd been vacillating between his feelings for Melody and getting the bill passed and he knew that there could only be one winner right now. It had to be the bill, but he wanted to be with Melody or someone who could make him feel the way she did, in his future.

She'd woken him up to the fact that he'd made a life for himself that was successful but solitary. Previously he'd been able to fool himself into believing that the choices he'd been making were the ones that would keep him happy or that he was being strategic in a way his father had never been.

But as of tonight that logic was no longer applicable. He wasn't saving himself heartache. He wasn't leaving relationship roadkill behind him. He was avoiding any real commitment because he was too afraid of ending up like his father. All that regret. All the loss his father had experienced from having the family that he dreamed of but never enjoying it.

"Thanks, Dad. You know I think if you showed Mom this side of you—"

"She'd take me back," August said. "I know. The thing is that in the past I never meant it. I said what I needed to in order to keep the beautiful wife that other men envied by my side. And now that I do mean it…is it too late?"

Was it?

Dare didn't know. But he was sure that his mom had never loved another man the way she loved August. "If you want to make it work, Dad, you can. I think you know that. Are you afraid that if you leave yourself truly vulnerable and she says no…"

He couldn't bring himself to say that his father wouldn't recover. August Bisset was the strongest, most ruthless man he'd ever met, and Dare didn't want to think of his father as having that deep a vulnerability. Dare wanted to believe that his parents could work things out without one of them hurting each other. But the truth was his father had been hurting his mom emotionally for so long that both

Dare and his dad saw a possibility that this time she might have reached her limit.

Dare's heart ached for his parents. He wanted to avoid this fate of being his father's age and alone and scared that he'd wasted his life. And a part of him wanted to believe that Melody could be the solution, but another part knew she wasn't. She was young and still had to figure out her life. Dare, on the other hand, had made mistakes, had triumphs and knew or thought he knew what he wanted for the future. It was the combination of seeing the cracks in his parents' marriage and this lust/like thing he had for Melody that was clouding his judgment. For a man known for his calm, solid reasoning, it was disarming and he didn't like it.

Eleven

"How did the meeting with Tad Williams go?" Johnny asked her the next morning in their stand-up meeting.

"It was interesting. I did see Senator Bisset and his father at the bar. They noticed me talking to Tad. Just so you are aware. But Tad has some women who'd like to testify against the bill before the committee. They're in Boston," Melody said. She'd spent the night working on her notes, which she had emailed to the team this morning.

She pushed a hard copy over to Johnny, who said he was old school and liked to read on paper. She waited until he reviewed her notes and then looked up at her. "This is good stuff. Book yourself a flight to Boston to get this testimony for us to use to begin our influence campaign on the senators. When the time comes we will have to have live testimony. Shawna will set you up with everything you need. I think video will be best and then send them to the transcriptionist, so we have it on paper, too."

"I will do that," she said.

She had to admit that after the stress of the last few weeks in DC she was looking forward to going to Boston. It was close enough to her parents' home on Martha's Vineyard that she knew her mom and dad would come and see her while she was there and, to be honest, she needed some pampering. Just to be around her parents who loved her even when she screwed up.

She left the meeting with a list of senators and lobbyists she had to call to get support but was a bit lighter at the thought of having a few days away from this. She contacted Tad Williams's office to set up the meetings, then notified Shawna that her return ticket would need to be for the following Thursday with an approved weekend stay.

"You're going to Boston? That's different," Aubrey said when Melody got back to their shared office. Chris was out doing some legwork on another project.

"We found some people willing to share their personal stories that will help support our case," Melody said. "Johnny asked me to go and conduct the interviews."

"You're certainly doing well here."

"Thanks," she said. "I think Johnny just needs to see you in action and then he will realize what a gem you are. Do you want to help me with some meetings today? If we conduct them together and jointly send in the notes...well, it couldn't hurt."

Aubrey looked over at her and then smiled. "You'd do that?"

"Yes. I know we all want to look good and do well here. Plus, you're sort of my only friend in DC," Melody said with a wink. As much as she wasn't into sharing glory, she did want to have a level playing field. She wasn't sure what had driven her to make the offer, but she was glad she did. She had been feeling isolated and alone, especially since she was the only one of the junior research staffers on the A-team at the firm.

"Great. What should I do to prepare?" Aubrey asked.

"We are talking to two senators who are on the fence. We need some hard facts and I haven't had a chance to do a deep dive on them both to find out what their hot buttons are. Maybe if I take one and you take the other, that will give us more time for a strategy session. I'll have to run this by Shawna, but I don't think she'll mind."

"Of course."

"Let's go and see her now," Melody said. A part of her wondered if she was offering Aubrey this chance to prove herself in front of Tad as a salve to her conscience. She still felt guilty from last night when she'd seen Dare and his dad at the bar. When Dare had seen her meeting with his family's rival. She knew she was being aboveboard and doing her job but still it had stung to realize that he wasn't ever going to see it that way. By putting the job first, she'd used him and everything she did was going to be filtered through that lens.

They went to see Shawna and she approved Aubrey working with her on the interviews during the day and even suggested that Aubrey go with her to Boston.

"Thanks for this," Aubrey said to Melody when they left Shawna's office. "I don't know how to repay you."

"It's okay. We're on the same team," Melody said. "I'm staying the weekend in Boston to visit my parents. I'm not sure if you can stay that long, but I'll forward my travel details to you if you want to try to book the same flight."

"I'm not sure about the weekend. I might need to get back to do some work. But thanks for the offer," Aubrey said.

Melody and Aubrey worked through the rest of the day together, going over to the Capitol building to conduct some more meetings and try to sway senators to vote against Dare's bill.

Most of the senators they spoke to were reluctant to give a firm answer one way or the other. It was a long and frustrating day.

"I need a double shot of espresso before we got to any other meetings," Aubrey said.

"Agreed."

They headed to the coffee shop and got in line when she noticed Dare and he noticed her. She tugged on Aubrey's sleeve and asked her to hold her place in line. She went over to talk to Dare.

"Hello," she said.

"Hi," he responded.

"About last night—"

"Don't mention it. This is DC and I know how the political game is played. It's only natural that you'd meet with the man who hates my family. I get it."

He sounded like he was ticked off. He might be speaking in a low tone so that their conversation didn't go any further than her ears. She got where he was coming from, but that was so unfair. "I can't talk now. Are you running later?" she asked.

"I am."

"See you then. I want to discuss this."

"What if I don't?"

She didn't want those words to hurt as much as they did. "Then I suppose you'll run somewhere else."

She turned and walked away from him to find Aubrey watching her. "Do you know Senator Bisset?"

"I met him at a wedding reception a few weeks ago," she said. "Obviously he's not happy that his family's business rival is helping us. That's all."

"How does he know?"

She was a bit annoyed that Aubrey was asking so many questions but just smiled. "I saw him at the bar where I met Tad Williams. I was hoping to smooth things over just now. Let's get back to work. We don't have time to waste."

She walked away from Aubrey—and from Dare—determined to move past this any way she could.

Dare watched Melody leave and regretted that he had to hold his tongue for now. He wasn't a man to do that ever, so this was difficult. For the first time since he met Melody, he had a real glimpse of how complicated things were between them. Sure he'd known the facts but watching her tense conversation with her coworker and then how she walked away, he knew that when he saw her tonight—and he was definitely going to meet her—he had to end this.

For her sake as much as his.

He didn't want to be sixtysomething like his dad and alone in a bar talking about regrets. He was actually at a point in his life where he was happy with all of the choices he'd made and the path that had brought him to where he was.

It didn't seem very smart to him to screw it up now. He was going to keep working on getting support for his bill, but he would delegate dealing with Johnny's team to Cami. He didn't need to be involved in those meetings, as much as he liked to be totally hands-on. In this case, he needed to pull back.

Though he was still ticked that Melody had talked

to Tad, he understood why she had and he was over it. It had stung at first…but only because he didn't want them to be rivals. That was why he had to end this. He was starting to lose his edge and make allowances that he normally wouldn't.

Tonight, he was going to use Tad as the reason why he wouldn't see her anymore. That was it. It would be over, and he'd move on.

His phone pinged and he glanced at the screen to see it was his cousin Adler calling.

"Hey. One second. I'm in the lobby at the Capitol. Let me get somewhere private. How's the honeymoon?"

"Hey. It's fine. We're cutting it short to head back to Gran's. She's volunteered her house as the meeting place for Nick and Logan to work out their differences and get this patent deal back on track. They're going to issue a joint statement to the press. Nick said he's sending you the information so you can be there," she said, sounding a little bit sad and resigned.

Adler was getting hit with the same curse that had followed his mom. Loving a man who let business consume him. Was Nick the same as August? The two men barely knew each other besides sharing some DNA. It was hard for Dare to think of Nick as his half brother, and Dare knew that the other man didn't want the Bissets as siblings. He had his own family, Nick had said.

"I'm sorry," Dare said.

"Yeah, it's fine," Adler responded.

"It's not. My father has regrets—"

"Don't, Dare. Don't make me start to think about forgiving Uncle Auggie when I'm really pissed at him. I'm not ready for that yet. I want him to pay for what he did. I want him to understand that his actions have repercussions and that I am not willing to let him skate on this," Adler said.

He agreed with her. Of course, the father that Dare had spoken with last night was a completely different man than the one who'd been so selfish and arrogant in his younger years. But that didn't change the fact that his dad had a lot of apologies he needed to make to their entire family.

"I get it. I'm mad for you, too. I hate that he ruined your wedding day for you," Dare said. "If your mom was alive, she would have blasted him. She never let him get away with anything."

"She didn't?" Adler asked. She was a baby when her mom had died, so she didn't have the memories that Dare did of Musette.

"No. She just didn't tolerate excuses from him. Mom was always forgiving him and doing whatever she had to in order to keep her husband, but your mom said…" Dare stopped, remembering how his aunt had told her sister that she should put herself first for once. That August was going to keep walking all over her until she did. Had his mom ever done that?

To Dare's memory it seemed like she'd always

put the family ahead of her own needs until Marielle was born.

"Dare?"

"She just said if you give him an inch, he'll walk all over you," he said. "Do you mind if I invite Dad to come to Gran's? I think everyone needs to tell him how they feel."

"I don't mind. I want this over. I want my Nick back and I want this mess to be behind us," Adler said. "I'm not sure that Uncle Auggie will come."

"He will," Dare promised. He would make sure of it. Because he remembered it was after his mom and Aunt Musette had had that conversation that she'd gotten pregnant, leading to Logan…and that had brought on another lie, but this time from his mom. There was such a mess in their past and it needed to be resolved so they could all move on.

"Thanks, Dare. I was calling just because I needed to talk to someone who was on my side," she said.

"I'm always on your side, Ad. Call any time," he reassured her.

"Thanks. Love you," she said.

"Love you, too," he responded, and then they hung up.

He stood there in the corner of the lobby thinking about how different Adler and Melody were but how they were both caught without their consent in the Bisset/Williams web of deceit. He was going to cut Melody out of it tonight. He knew that he'd miss her, because even last night while she'd been meeting with Tad Williams all he'd been able to do was wish she'd been there with him.

But he didn't have time for her, as much as he might wish it were different. He had his hands full getting his bill passed and being the only one who could bring peace between the Bisset and Williams families. He didn't need the distraction that Melody provided. As much as he might want it.

The foot traffic near the Lincoln Monument was heavy that evening but Melody had no problem spotting Dare. He hadn't brought Bailey with him, which she thought was telling.

He was going to break up with her.

Wasn't that what she wanted? Wasn't she helping Aubrey out instead of taking all the kudos for herself to make up for what she'd done with Dare?

Sure, she was upset that she never had the chance to explore the relationship that could have been, but breaking up made more sense.

He waved at her as he approached, and she went over to him. "Glad you showed."

"Yeah. I figured we needed to talk and this is pretty much the only place where we can."

"I know. Listen, about last night—"

"You don't have to explain yourself, " he said, cutting her off. "You're working to stop my bill and it makes sense to talk to Tad Williams. He's probably got a dossier of things my family has done to hurt the little guy."

She almost smiled at the way Dare said it. It hadn't been lost on Melody that Tad wasn't fond of the Bisset family. But that meeting hadn't felt personal; maybe she'd read Tad wrong. "I don't want to hurt your ego but we weren't focused on you or your family one time."

Dare put his hand over his heart and staggered back as if he'd been wounded. "What? Does this mean the world doesn't revolve around me?"

"I mean, maybe," she said. "Don't let it get you down. You're still number one in a lot of people's books."

"Thanks. Am I in yours?" he asked.

"Dare."

"I know. I'm here to end this. I imagine you are, too," he said. "But when I'm with you it's so much harder to walk away than I thought it would be."

"For me, too," she admitted. "You are so magnetic in person. When you're here in running clothes just being just you, not the official you, it's different."

"When you walked away today, I felt like an idiot. I know who you work for. I know this job is incredibly important to you and it should be. But at the same time, there is a part of me that feels like you are mine. That you shouldn't be talking to anyone in the Williams family. And before you say it I know it's the twenty-first century and that women don't belong to men…but my gut says differently. My gut wants to grab your hand and take you back to my place."

"For tonight?" she asked. She wanted that, too.

She wanted to belong to him, which was so not her. She was her own woman and had been for a long time, but this was Dare. The man who haunted her dreams and could turn her on just by standing next to her. He was funny and smart and all these things that she'd noted in other men but somehow when it all combined in Dare's body it was what she'd been looking for.

Even though she hadn't been looking.

Even though he was the wrong man for her.

Even though she knew that no matter when they ended things, they would eventually be over for good.

"Yes," he said. "Maybe for longer."

"Longer?"

He nodded.

"You have to say more than that, Dare. Longer like the weekend? Or a few months?" she asked. Because if she followed this wild impulse and did give in to it, she had to know what she was risking everything for. A weekend wasn't worth it. But then again, could she just walk away from him?

She wanted to believe she could, but another part of her wasn't too sure.

"I don't know. I've never been a long-term guy. But I've never felt about a woman the way I feel about you," he said.

And that told her nothing and yet everything. Her heart beat a little bit faster. She could feel his body heat and smell the scent of his aftershave. She'd missed him, which in her head made no sense since she'd slept with him twice and maybe spent less than twenty-four hours total with him. But her heart…her heart said this wasn't over and urged her to do whatever she had to in order to keep him in her arms.

"So, what are you saying?" she asked.

"Am I enough for you? I can't make promises because I won't be like my dad, who has always broken them to the people he cares about," Dare said.

"Then don't break them. Just do what you can do," she said.

It was so hard to read the expression in his light blue eyes as he stared down at her. She saw his jaw tighten and felt his conflict radiating from him in a wave. He struggled and it made her want to just accept what he could give her.

But her integrity wouldn't let her accept that. She might be young but she knew her worth and if Dare thought she didn't…well, she couldn't let him take everything she had while offering only a little bit of himself. He had to meet her all the way or it wasn't worth it.

"I can't do this if you're not going to be all in. I'm not asking you to promise me forever, but I need to know that I matter for more than some hot sex and that you are willing to really try to make this work." There. She'd put her heart on the line and if he said no, it would hurt. No use denying that. But she'd know where she stood. And she could move on.

"Wow. I can't believe how honest you are," he said.

She waited to see if he was going to continue but he didn't.

"So no?"

"So yes," he said, pulling her into his arms and kissing her.

Twelve

Yes.

She felt a little thrill go through her. Yet at the same time how was this going to work?

She pulled back from him, aware they were in public and kissing probably wasn't a great idea. But she wanted him. She wanted to be his woman and stand by his side, except...again, how?

"Second thoughts?" he asked, giving her some distance and turning to stare at the tourists moving around them.

"No. But how does this work?"

"We need to figure that out. I'm heading to Nantucket during the recess and would love for you to join me if you can. I know that you can't take the entire three weeks off but I rented my own house on

Nantucket, so it's not like we'll be with my family though they will be there. We can take some time to get to know each other and work out the logistics of this," he said.

Nantucket. Not that far from her parents who were on Martha's Vineyard for the summer. "I was planning to be at my parents' this weekend in Martha's Vineyard. I think we could make it for this weekend. And then I could come up for the Labor Day."

"That's great. I'm taking my own plane to Nantucket if you want a ride," he offered.

"Generous, but I'm going to Boston on business first," she said. "I'll rent a car and then—"

"Let me pick you up in Boston," he offered. "I can take you to your parents' and leave my car with you and then get the ferry to Nantucket."

He was trying, she could see that. She liked the idea of seeing him sooner. "My business is done on Friday night."

"Great. Would you like to go out for dinner and then we can drive to your folks on Saturday morning?" he asked. "My brother has a place in Boston that I can use."

"I'd love that. There is a new restaurant in Collins Commons I'm dying to try."

"Good, then it's a plan. Send me your hotel details and I'll meet you there," he said.

She smiled over at him. "Are we doing this?"

"Yes, we are. I hesitated earlier because my track record with relationships isn't great, but I can't stop thinking about you, Melody. I want this to be more than just the two nights we've had together."

"Me, too," she admitted. "Where did you stash Bailey?"

"I left him at home, and he wasn't too happy about it," Dare admitted. "I promised to bring him back some ice cream though I doubt that will be enough for him to forgive me."

"It was a bit mean leaving him behind. Why did you?" she asked.

"I was going to end things with you, and Bailey likes you, so it would have been harder," he admitted.

Her heart softened a little more toward him. No matter what she'd read about his hardline stance on certain issues, she could tell that when he cared he did it one hundred percent.

"I'm glad, then. It would have been harder for me, too," she admitted. "I haven't really done much running. Wanna do another lap with me and then we can get ice cream before you head home?"

He looked over at her and she felt things that she struggled to categorize. Emotions that were new and foreign, and that she wasn't too sure she trusted. She got the lust thing. Dare was superhot and exactly her type with his muscular arms and lean, athletic frame. And those icy blue eyes got to her every time. But the other bit, this affection? Was that what it was?

He nodded, then winked at her. "Loser buys."

He started running and she dashed after him. He got her. Not that she'd been super subtle when she'd tried to outrun him at the end last time, but a lot of guys wouldn't have noticed and Dare had.

Despite his challenge, for the bulk of the run he kept pace next to her, weaving around tourists. Only as they both spotted the ice cream vendor that was their finish line did the pace pick up. She started to push herself. She knew that the running in place she'd done in her apartment had helped but she still wasn't on Dare's level. So she was surprised when she beat him by a pace and a half.

She gave him a hard look. "Did you let me win?"

He shook his head. "You are just really fast."

"Ha. I'll have pralines and cream," she said. "Meet you over there."

She walked away from Dare and felt his gaze on her as she did so. He was watching her. She glanced back over her shoulder and felt a bolt of pure sensual awareness shoot through her when he mouthed that he wanted her.

Me, too, she mouthed back.

But they both knew that it was too risky to go to each other's place in DC again until they'd figured out this thing between them. Melody realized that for her it would almost be easy to risk it. To give up all the momentum she was building with Johnny and his team. And that made her pause.

She'd give it up for Dare?

That wasn't like her. She was a strong, driven woman who had her life planned out, and that meant career first and men later, in her thirties. Had she made a huge misstep with him?

Probably.

Was she going to change her mind?

She got to the bench and looked back over at him where he was talking to a family who was behind him in line for the ice cream. She knew in her heart that she wasn't going to change her mind unless he did something to make her reevaluate how she felt about him.

And though her emotions were foreign and strange, a part of her knew she was falling in love with him. She'd never been in love before and it scared her more than she wanted to admit.

Leaving DC had been easy, knowing he'd get to have some private time with Melody over the weekend. He'd decided to fly out on Thursday to get a jump on the weekend and spend some time with his youngest brother, Zac, who would be leaving for Australia to start training for the America's Cup in two weeks. Zac had gotten engaged to Iris Collins. Dare hadn't expected his outdoorsy brother to fall for a woman as polished and sophisticated as Iris but Dare knew that opposites attract. Hell, that had to be what was happening with him and Melody.

She was different. He'd known that from the moment he'd found her at the entrance of the wedding reception. But it was more than that. There were times when as much as he was afraid to commit to her, he could see them both growing old together.

He shook his head and shoved that thought out of his mind as he got out of his private plane and walked toward the hangar. He saw Zac leaning on the hood of Gran's '69 Camaro. It was a sporty car; to be honest it was really difficult for Dare to picture his grandmother driving something that flashy, but they all were glad she had it.

Zac waved at him and stood up, walking toward him to hug him. Dare hugged his little brother back. "I'm getting too used to seeing you. Is there any chance you'd give up your dream and move back?"

"Yes, but not for you," Zac said with a laugh. "Iris and I are talking about the future and I think this might be my last run in the Cup."

"Really?" Dare asked. "Are you sure?"

He'd been half joking with Zac, who had always been more at home on the sea than on land. But his brother had grown up. Dare knew that all of them had, and this latest trouble with their father had served to force them to lean on each other, strengthening the bond that had always existed between them.

"Yeah. Iris has some ideas and that woman is great at innovating ways to reach an audience. She's even talking about involving Leo and having him and Danni design some merchandise for the venture. She sees me doing yachting weekends for couples or small groups."

"You want that?" Dare asked again. Because Zac was a great guy and everyone loved him, but honestly, Dare knew a big part of the reason why Zac took to the sea was to get away from people.

"No. But I want her to be happy."

"Z, this is just my opinion, but if you're not happy she won't be, either. Don't do it for her, do it because of her. Find your own path," Dare said. "And also remember, I'm single, so take my advice with a grain of salt."

"Still single? I heard that you and the blonde from the reception were getting close," Zac said.

"Who'd you hear that from?" he asked.

"Dad. Believe it or not he's been here since Monday. Just listening and running errands for Gran and Mom. Mom got here on Tuesday. I've never seen Dad like this," he said.

"Like what?"

"Humble," Zac said with a laugh.

"Yeah, right," Dare said.

"No, really. It's like he's suddenly realized what we knew all along," Zac said.

"What's that?"

"That we are an awesome family and now he wants to be a part of it," Zac said. "But no one is making it easy on him. It's not like we haven't tried this in the past and seen what happens."

"Exactly," Dare said. "For what it's worth I had drinks with him in DC and he does seem to genuinely want to change this time."

"Yeah, I think so, too," Zac said. "Part of my problem with the thing with Iris is that I've seen Dad put himself first for years, and as much as I want to find a post-Cup career that will be fulfilling for me, I don't want to be Dad."

Wasn't that the mantra for all the Bisset boys? Their father was so dynamic and successful, a man many envied, and yet his sons didn't want to follow in his footsteps, not really.

Dare clapped his hand on Zac's shoulder and looked into his brother's blue eyes. "You won't be. You've always been more like Mom."

"I can't believe you're still calling me a mama's boy."

Dare laughed because he hadn't done that, but Zac always had been a mama's boy. As the baby, Zac had gotten away with just about everything. It had been irritating when they were younger but now it made them both smile.

"If the shoe fits."

"Ha. Let's get going. Mom's expecting us for lunch," Zac said. They walked to the car and Zac stopped before getting in. "Hey, thanks for the advice. I just don't want to screw this up. Iris is the best thing that's ever happened to me."

"You won't," he reassured his brother, realizing as they drove though Nantucket that he was starting to feel that Melody was the best thing to happen to him.

Or that she could be if he found a way to stop

fearing commitment and let her know that she mattered to him in his life.

"Oh, Mom said you're going to Boston on Friday. Do you mind if I catch a ride with you? Iris's parents are taking us out to dinner to celebrate our engagement."

"I don't mind at all," he said. Their lives were all moving on, he thought. His could, too, if he'd just take the chance and reach out and take what he wanted. But that had always been the hardest thing for him to do.

The interviews with the women Tad Williams had put Melody in touch with went really well. Their stories had been heartfelt and moving. They also wouldn't benefit from some after-purchase rebate or flat fee prescription drugs because their children had rare diseases, and the government funding to pharmaceutical companies helped in research and development of new medicines for this. Rare diseases needed to be considered in his new bill. Melody was sure that once she brought this to Johnny he'd be able to use it. But a crucial piece of information that no one in the lobbying group had been aware of had been brought to their attention by Cora Williams.

She mentioned that the first woman—Blanche Jones—had gone to talk to the committee when Dare's predecessor had been in charge. And no one had called her back. She was not too happy with the form letter she'd received or the fact that she'd been treated so poorly. Her son had a chronic illness that was rare, and only through the trials run by a big pharmaceutical company was he getting any help.

Blanche Jones made it clear that she thought the Senate committee didn't care about families like hers. She said that they were only interested in making a big grand gesture that would spell the end of programs such as the one she was benefiting from.

Melody had had to bite her tongue to keep from jumping to Dare's defense, but in the end she couldn't just let the woman walk away thinking that he wouldn't listen to her story. Which wasn't like her. She kept her head down and made a lot of notes. But she knew that it was damning that no one on the committee had gotten back to Blanche. Anyone with a heart would have at least called her.

She wasn't sure how to handle this. She couldn't give Dare a heads-up. That would be an ethical breach. But she couldn't help thinking that if he did know he'd make this right.

And then what?

She worked for Johnny and not Dare. Dare was a senator and hopefully had been doing his research for the bill he was sponsoring. She wondered if he would have spoken to any of the women she had, due to his family conflict with Tad Williams.

No matter what happened between the two of them personally she had to remember that. Yet at the same time, Johnny was doing this to help people like Blanche. He wasn't in there trying to defeat Dare because he was a Bisset. And not that it mattered to anyone else, but Cora Williams was a really nice lady who wanted both low prescription medicine costs and people like Blanche to get the help they needed from the government. It made no sense to keep funneling money into drug research if mothers like Blanche weren't able to the assistance they needed, which could only come from the government funds that were provided to pharmaceutical companies.

"That went well," Aubrey said after their last interview. "I'm surprised at how angry they were. I'll tell you I always thought maybe I'd have kids when I was older but now I'm rethinking it. I don't know if I could go through what those families have."

Melody felt the same. There was enough uncertainty in relationships in this day and age, she couldn't imagine what would happen if she were in that situation with Dare. And they were no longer together.

Would he leave her with his child?

She had the feeling deep inside that he wouldn't. That Dare Bisset would honor his commitment to their child if they had one.

Which sent her down a road of thoughts she shouldn't be thinking. What would their child look like? She pictured children with his black hair and her brown eyes playing with Bailey.

"Melody?"

"Sorry, what?" *Snap out of it, girl.*

"I asked if you wanted to grab a drink in the bar at the hotel tonight. I know you have plans but my flight isn't until later, so I have some time."

"I wish I could," Melody said. "But I have a date."

"A date? I didn't realize you were from Boston," Aubrey said. "I assume it's a boy from here."

"He's a man, actually," Melody said with a wink but at the same time it was the truth. No one would refer to Dare as a boy.

"Ha. So he's from Boston?"

"New York," Melody said. "I met him while I was at my parents' cottage in Cape Cod. We are going to grab dinner since we are both back for the weekend."

"Ooo. Long-distance love. It can be so hot, am I right? It's like you get to experience all the best parts of being in a relationship and none of the mundane. When it's just a weekend you don't have to put up with any bad habits and he doesn't have to know about yours."

Melody hadn't thought of it that way. "You're right. But it's sort of lonely, too. Knowing you like someone but can't be with them…it's an odd feeling."

"Odd in what way? Do you love him?" Aubrey asked.

Melody shrugged. It was a question she'd been trying to answer for herself. "I don't know. Like you said, it's just hot and exciting. But there's no time to explore the relationship, you know?"

"I'm sorry," Aubrey said. "But I guess if you both feel that way then it will change."

"I hope so," Melody admitted.

They finished working on the press release about the women they'd interviewed to generate some public support for defeating Dare's bill and emailed it to Constance to send out next week. "Good. That's all done," Aubrey said.

"Let's go back to the hotel. Sorry I can't meet you for a drink."

"That's okay. We can celebrate back in DC."

"Yes," Melody agreed.

They said goodbye in the lobby. Melody was glad that Aubrey was heading to the airport and back to DC so she wouldn't risk running into her when she was with Dare. Melody rushed upstairs to get changed and touch up her makeup before going back down to meet Dare. He was waiting near the concierge desk when she walked off the elevators. Her heart beat faster and she felt happy all over when he smiled at her. And no matter what doubts she might have thought she had, she knew she was in love with Dare Bisset.

Whatever else was going on in her life, she was totally certain that she wanted him in it. But how was she going to make it work? She wasn't sure how much information to share with him, or if he would ask about her meetings. It was unnerving to try to balance this side of their relationship.

He took her hand and led her to a private alcove. "I've been waiting to do this all day," he said.

He pulled her into his arms and kissed her long

and deep before taking her hand in his and leading her out of the lobby. "I like being able to do that. Not having to worry that someone from my office or Johnny's will see us."

"Me, too," she admitted. She linked her hand in his. As they moved from the alcove into the lobby, she thought she felt someone watching her and glanced around, then dropped Dare's hand as she met Aubrey's gaze.

She felt a moment of trepidation. Would Aubrey rat her out? She hoped her friend wouldn't.

Thirteen

Melody was freaking out on the inside but kept a calm smile as Dare drove them not toward Collins Commons but the harbor. Should she text Johnny? "I hope you don't mind but I have a surprise," Dare said, interrupting her thoughts.

"What kind of surprise?" she asked.

"My brother offered us his yacht for the evening, and I hired a private chef to cook for us. One of Zac's sailing friends is going to pilot us around the harbor while we dine. This way we can have some privacy."

She liked that. She wondered if she should mention that Aubrey had seen them. Did that matter? She hoped her coworker knew that Melody wasn't reporting on their meetings that day to Dare. He could read about the work they'd done like everyone else in the press release or when Johnny sent him a briefing.

"That sounds nice."

"You okay?" he asked. "You seem distracted. Do you need to go back to the hotel so you can finish working?"

"No, it's nothing like that. I think a colleague of mine saw us together," she said.

"Oh. Well, that's not ideal. I should have been more cautious when I saw you. I'm surprised it happened here and not in DC. Do you need to talk to her?"

Melody just hadn't figured out how she was going to manage this. "I'm not sure. Let me text her, okay?"

"Sure, take all the time you need," Dare said, turning away to give her some privacy.

She typed out several messages to Aubrey but deleted them as they weren't right. Finally she just texted, I didn't mean to put you in an awkward position. Dare and I agreed to catch up for a drink. I told you we met at the wedding. I hope you understand.

Sure. I'm on my way to the airport. Talk soon.

Melody felt like she was reading too much into the text but she wasn't sure about Aubrey. She wished she'd double-checked her coworker had left the hotel before going down to meet Dare. But she couldn't go back and undo it.

And she wasn't embarrassed by her relationship

with him. She put the matter out of her head for now. There was nothing for her to worry about at this moment. She had to wait and see what Aubrey did.

"It was nice of Zac to offer his boat," Melody said to get his attention.

"It was," Dare agreed. "I was struggling to come up with a way for us to avoid anything awkward in public but if you're friend saw us maybe it won't matter."

"I don't know," she admitted. "We were planning to discuss, this so that is something we should address. I'm going to have to let Johnny know. I hope that Aubrey—that's my coworker—doesn't spill it before I can."

Dare glanced over at her as he braked to stop for the traffic light. "Are you worried?"

She shrugged, but of course she was. Aubrey was competitive like her and there was no denying that if Melody had been sitting on this kind of information about a colleague she didn't measure up against, she'd use it to her advantage. "A bit."

"What can I do?"

Nothing. But she knew he wanted to help and appreciated that. "Just distract me tonight."

"Can do," he said.

When they got to the marina and boarded his brother's yacht, Melody put Aubrey out of her mind. The sky was clear and bright and the evening warm but not too hot. This was her first real date with Dare unless she counted those two runs and dinner at his house. But this was different.

A table had been set up for them on the deck. Dare led her to the railing and they watched the city go by as the boat left the marina and went out into the harbor.

He stood behind her, his arms wrapped around her, and Melody rested against him, letting her fears and worries seep away. She knew they'd be waiting for her when she got back to shore, but for this moment she wanted to just enjoy being with Dare.

To see if the risk she'd taken was worth it. She thought it was but there was always the fear that maybe he was playing a game to make up for the one she'd played when they met.

"This is nice. My brother and I used to race on one-person sailboats when we were younger," Melody said. "It's been a while since I've been out on a boat."

"Really? We spend a lot of time sailing as a family. I don't do as much as my brothers, but then I don't live on the water…not really. And I like it better when someone else is piloting the boat so I can just enjoy it."

"Yeah. What else do you enjoy?" she asked. This night wasn't just about deciding if they could make this work. She wanted to get to know as much about Dare as she could. She wanted these memories to keep in case it didn't work.

"Well, running, as you know" he said. "Do you enjoy it?"

"No. I do it, but I wouldn't say I enjoy it," she said with a laugh. "But I like it when I go with you and Bailey. Did you bring him with you this weekend?"

"No. I have to go back to DC on Monday for a meeting and then I'll bring him up for the rest of the summer. Cami watches him for me when I'm gone."

Cami.

His pretty assistant.

"Was there something between the two of you?"

"No. She's always just been a friend," he said. "Jealous?"

"Maybe. I mean, she's got a lot more in common with you than I do," she said.

"She works for me," he said. "I've never been comfortable dating someone in my office. Just seems like a scandal waiting to happen. Plus, all of my dad's affairs were with women he worked with."

Interesting. So Dare had shied away because he didn't think that the office was a good place to start a romance. "I'm sorry about your dad."

"Me, too. He's been trying to change...well, for the three weeks since the wedding and everything blowing up," Dare said.

"I hope he does," she said.

"What do you enjoy?" he asked, changing the subject.

She thought about it. She didn't have a lot of time for hobbies. "I guess reading. I have a stack of books that I've purchased and haven't had time to read yet, though."

"Workaholic," he teased.

"Sort of. The thing is, this is a new job, so I want to make a good impression."

"Believe me I know you do," he said.

She turned in his arms and looked up into his blue eyes. "Are we good about that?"

"Yes. I was being...sarcastic. Sorry, I guess maybe I'm not as over it as I want to be," he admitted.

"I get it. It's hard to trust someone who's betrayed you, isn't it?" she asked.

"Yes. Harder than I thought it would be. And I don't think of what you did as betrayal," he said.

But she knew it was. She wondered if anything good could come from a lie. She doubted it. And that made her sad because she had the feeling that Dare was the kind of man she would have enjoyed sharing her life with.

Dare cursed himself for bringing that up. But it served to remind him that he still wasn't sure of her motives. Even the fact that she was worried that a co-worker had seen them together was another red flag.

And as much as he hoped to find a way forward for them as a couple, he couldn't help wondering if they'd be better off apart. Zac was struggling to find his footing in a relationship with Iris that was infinitely less complicated than what he and Melody had going on, which made Dare concerned that they'd ever be able to work this out.

Melody was at the beginning of a career that she had admitted she loved. She'd also just told him that she lived for her job and had no hobbies. He got it. He remembered being in his early twenties and thinking that work was everything. But he was older now. And maybe a bit wiser, though tonight he didn't really feel that way. Tonight he just wished there was some way he could forget how they'd met and how she was on the opposite side of the issues from him.

But there wasn't. He suddenly had an inkling of why his mom had taken his dad back so many times. The fact that he wanted to delude himself into thinking there was a way forward for him and this young woman should be a red flag.

"What are you thinking?" she asked.

"That I wish you'd just been a Toby Osborn fan and nothing more when I met you at the wedding," he said.

"Me, too," she admitted. "Though I never would have crashed it if it hadn't been for you."

There it was.

They only met because of his job and who he was. He was going to have to find a way around this or he was going to have to walk away. He knew it, and given the way she was looking at him, he suspected she did, too.

"Let's go sit down. I asked the chef to start serving our appetizers when we were out of the main marina," he said.

He put his hand on the small of her back to steady her as they walked. She felt small and feminine under his touch and he was reminded that it had been too long since he'd held her in his arms. Too long since he'd kissed her. He slipped his hand around her waist to stop her and pulled her into an embrace, kissing her as if this night might be their last together. Because reality was intruding and he could no longer pretend there was any scenario where he could make this work.

No matter how much he wanted to.

She put her arms around him and kissed him back with the same passion and edginess that he felt flowing through his body. It was as if they both realized that this was their last night together.

Dare hated that the moment he'd found a woman he wanted to build a future with, his career made that impossible.

There was no denying that if it hadn't been for his career, he would never have met her. And he couldn't keep her for the same reason.

He lifted her in his arms and carried her past the table laid out with food to the stairs leading down into the sleeping quarters. He set her on her feet. "Do you want to—"

"Yes. Which way is the bedroom?"

He smiled at her direct way of speaking. There was so much about Melody that suited him on so many levels. He took her hand in his and led the way to the master bedroom. It had a full-size bed and a small porthole that allowed in some light. He closed the door behind them and pulled her back into his arms.

He kissed her, slowly and deeply. Taking his time and making it last. Her hands were moving over him, undoing the buttons of his shirt and shoving it off his shoulders. He shrugged out of it and her hands were on his chest, tracing over the padded muscles and following the line of hair that tapered down his stomach. He felt her hand slip into the front of his pants and her fingers rubbing over his erection.

He groaned and reached down to undo his pants. Then he cupped her butt and drew her into his arms, falling with her onto the bed and pulling her on top of him. She straddled him and leaned over him, her hair falling on either side of his face as she kissed him and rubbed herself against him.

He undid the buttons at the front of her dress and pushed it open to cup her breasts, his fingers twirling over her nipples as his tongue thrust deeper into her mouth. She braced herself with one hand on his chest and shimmied out of her panties before she came back to straddle him again.

He felt her moist center rubbing against his shaft. Then she shifted, and he reached down to steady himself as the tip of his cock entered her body. He put his hands on her hips as she took him completely. She rode him, taking the entire length of his cock inside her. Her head fell back, her breasts thrusting forward toward his face. He suckled one nipple as she continued to move on him. She tightened around him, and then she cried out his name as she came. He thrust up inside of her harder, anchoring her hips to his with his hands as he finally reached his orgasm soon after hers.

She fell down on top of him, and he wrapped his arms around her and held her. Neither of them spoke. In his soul he was afraid this was goodbye. That her friend seeing them together and just the logistics of her job and his made this impossible. He wished there was another way for this to work out. But she was young and had a promising career in front of her. He'd seen how DC treated women in affairs with men and he wanted better for Melody. Wanted more for her. So if that meant he had break this off, he would.

He couldn't alienate her from her friends or cause her to lose her job. He wouldn't do that to Melody. He'd finally met a woman he wanted to give up everything for, but it was too late.

Melody lay on Dare's chest for as long as she could. Her heart was racing, and she wasn't sure where to go from here. She was worried about Aubrey. In her mind everything had become jumbled and she remembered how much easier this had been when they were apart.

When she was with him, he overwhelmed her

senses and made her think about a future that wasn't in her plans. A future she didn't have all mapped out and ready to go. A future she had no idea how to make a reality.

How could she move forward balancing a relationship with him and her career? Her parents worked in different fields, so the only personal example she had to go on was vastly different.

She rolled off him as she felt tears burning in the back of her eyes. She didn't want to end this but honestly how had she thought it could continue?

Aubrey's face had said it all. And she was just another researcher at the office. What would Johnny say? She knew that she had no way forward with Dare and she needed to end this. Make it a clean break so that she could try to get over him.

She'd never fallen in love before and now she was going to be dealing with her first broken heart.

It already hurt. She was already a mess inside trying to find the words to say what she needed to.

She sat up and looked over at him and one look at his face told her he already knew what had to happen.

"So, this is it," she said.

"You tell me," he said.

She realized that she had so much more to risk than he did. He was in a higher position than she was. He was a man and no matter how many strides they were making after the #MeToo movement, most would side with him if their affair was made public.

She knew that Dare would hate that, but it wouldn't help her.

"Don't do that," she said. "At least be honest. It's not just me saying goodbye. You are, too." She knew she was getting angry and most of the anger was at the situation. At the world they lived in that made it impossible for them to be together. But she was also a little bit ticked at Dare because he was being so neutral about it.

"I am," he said.

"Really? It seems like you are letting me make the decision and then just going along. Is it because you don't care or because you always knew it would end this way?" she asked, pushing herself off the bed and doing up the buttons of her blouse. She glanced around on the floor next to the bed for her underwear and shoved them in the pocket of her dress. She was still wearing her shoes.

She'd never made love like that. It had been intense. Something more than sex. But she knew now that it was less than the love she'd hoped for. She'd fooled herself into believing that this was going to be the start of something new. Now she had to wonder if he'd planned on it being the end all along.

"I care," he said, getting to his feet. "A lot. But I know that you are young and your job is the first step to a career for you. I don't want to be the reason you lose it."

"That's not going to happen. We haven't done anything that would put either of our jobs in jeopardy."

He gave her a sad smile. "You say that now but the truth is, Johnny and his team might not see it that way. There is a good chance if your coworker tells everyone back in the office she saw you with me, there will be some fallout."

She took a deep breath. This was it, she thought. The moment when she had a choice to make, and was she going to follow the path she always had? Say goodbye to Dare and the new feelings he evoked in her? Or was she going to take a chance?

"I don't want this to end." There, she'd said what was in her heart. And depending on his answer she'd know what she needed to do next.

"Me, neither," he admitted. "But I don't want you to regret being with me. I've seen what that looks like with my parents and it's not pretty."

"You're not your dad and I'm certainly not your mom. Believe me if you ever cheated on me I wouldn't be calmly standing next to you a cocktail party."

Dare laughed. "I'm glad to hear that. I wouldn't cheat. I can't do that."

She got it. His father had been having affairs throughout his son's life and it had shaped Dare into the man he was today. The man she knew she was falling in love with.

"So, what now?"

"Well, let's take the weekend like we planned and then we can fly back to DC on Sunday evening together. Do you want to come with me on my private plane?"

"Yes. I think I'm going to try to call Johnny tomorrow. I want to give him a heads-up about us. Is it okay to tell him?" she asked.

"Of course. I don't want to give him the impression that we've been sneaking around."

"Neither do I," she said, then let out a long breath. "I can't believe I'm doing this."

"Doing what?"

"Starting a relationship with you."

"I'm going to do everything I can to make sure you don't regret it," he said, pulling her back into his arms.

His words gave her pause but she shoved the niggling doubt out of her mind. What would she regret?

Dare made love to her again, which left no room for thinking or doubts. She was immersed in what being his woman was going to be like. He made her dinner and had her laughing as she cuddled next to him on the deck of the yacht.

The night deepened. He squeezed her close in his arms and she felt like out of all the chances she'd taken with Dare committing to a relationship with him was going to be most rewarding.

Fourteen

Dare arrived on Nantucket after leaving Melody at the ferry terminal from where she was going on to Martha's Vineyard. He missed her already. He thought that might be what Zac had been talking about when he said that he wanted to be closer to Iris. Dare had finally met a woman who didn't need him to be there for her all the time and he liked that, but at the same time, he wanted her to stay by his side.

Logan was waiting for him when the ferry landed. His brother looked tired and stressed, which he should be. But at the same time, he hated to see any of his siblings like this. Logan waved him over and he noticed that Quinn was with him. The two of them had been a couple in college and then broken up before getting back together at Adler's wedding. Quinn had been covering the event for a televised special.

"Hiya," Dare said. "Thanks for coming to meet me. But you didn't have to."

"He knows. He did it to escape your grandmother's house. She's not very happy with him," Quinn said as Dare hugged her.

Dare turned to hug his brother. "She'll be happier once you fix this."

"I know, but to fix it I have to make nice with Nick. We started making some progress at the wedding but I'm still not thrilled to be dealing with him and I'm not sure he's ready to, either," Logan said.

"Or you're not," Quinn said.

The spunky redhead kept his brother real, which Dare liked. "You both are ready for this because you both are starting to build lives that don't focus on beating each other in business."

"True," Logan said. "I do feel bad about what I did."

"I know," Dare said. All of the Bisset siblings reacted from the gut, often without thinking things through. But when they came to their senses, they always fixed things. "You'll make it right. Have you thought about how you will do that?"

"I have, actually. I've smoothed out the kinks in the patent deal. So that's taken care of—ownership will be transferred to Nick's company almost on the original schedule. But I had another idea that might be a better way of healing the rift between our families. I talked to Quinn about it on the way up here," he started.

"It's a good idea," Quinn said.

That was a promising sign. Logan outlined a plan to help bring the Bissets and Williamses together in the new venture. It was risky because Dare knew that his father would be up in arms about it. Hell, he wasn't too sure that Tad or Nick Williams would go for it, either. This was Logan at his most contrite and big-hearted. It made Dare proud of the man his brother was.

"This will work. We need to think of who should be in charge," Dare said.

"I was thinking Olivia Williams. Nick's sister. She's levelheaded and she reminds me of Leo—she's hungry but hasn't found her own business yet the way he has."

"I like that idea. In fact, that might be the key to winning Nick and his father over. Now it's just Dad we have to worry about."

"Dad will agree. I've already talked to him. He wants to make up for everything," Logan said.

"Okay, then, let's go and face the family," Dare said.

Michael, their grandmother's butler, showed them into the sitting room where Adler and Nick were waiting. But surprisingly, so were both of his parents. Dare hugged his mom and his dad before turning to Adler.

"Good to see you, kiddo. You look tan and happy," he said.

"Thanks. I was until you interrupted my honey-moon," Adler said. "I'm still not too happy about that."

"I'm sorry. But I didn't want you to get another nasty surprise."

"I am, too," Logan said. "And I think I have a plan to fix this."

"I'm listening," Nick said.

Adler's husband hadn't gotten up to greet them when they came in but he did wave and smile at Quinn. It was clear that Nick wasn't feeling friendly toward Dare or Logan despite the fact that they all now knew they were related, and that Logan was actually Nick's twin.

"I'm prepared to transfer the patent to you—I worked out the snags in the transaction and we can close the deal next week. But I have another idea. I think it's time for our families to find ways to build bridges between us, and we could turn my dick move into something positive," Logan said and paused for a long breath. "What do you say we form a limited company together to share the patent and the profits?"

"And we both try to comanage it?" Nick asked.

"No. There's no way we are there yet," Logan said. "But I want us to get there someday. My thought was that we'd co-own it. I've already paid for the patent, so you wouldn't have to put up much capital, just something to cover part of the operating costs. We'd hire someone else to run it—it wouldn't be one of us. And I have someone I think would be ideal."

"I'll need some time to come up with candidates as well," Nick said.

Dare almost smiled. Despite the fact that Nick and Logan were twins they were still used to being adversaries and one-upping each other.

"Well, my candidate is your sister, Olivia."

"Oh. Really?" Nick said. His brow furrowed in thought, and then he nodded. "I like it. In fact, there's no need to continue this discussion with everyone. Why don't you and I go and hash out the details and then give her a call?"

Nick stood up then and held his hand out to Logan, who took it and shook it. And Adler and Quinn both looked over at each other and smiled, clearly happy to see their men finally not being so stubborn with each other.

Dare watched them both leave and then turned to his parents. His father looked content and Dare knew he wouldn't fight this. He wanted peace for all of his sons, even the one he'd never known.

His mom put her hand over her mouth and looked as if she was about to cry when she stood up and left the room. Dare followed her.

"Mom, are you okay?"

She stopped and turned to him. "No…yes. I'm just so happy to see them getting along and finally building something between the Bisset and Williams families. And I wonder why your father could never have done that."

"Because I was a fool, Jules. I was too busy proving I was better than everyone else to see that," August said, following them into the hallway.

"You were a fool, but I was, too. I mean, look at them together. Did I do—" Their mother clearly still felt terrible guilt about keeping the secret of how Logan had been switched at birth, replacing her stillborn child.

"Nothing," August said. "This was all on me. And I will spend the rest of my life trying to prove that to you. I love you, Jules, and I hope you'll be able to forgive me soon."

"I already have," his mom admitted. "I just couldn't forgive myself."

"There's nothing to forgive," Dare said. "Dad is right about that."

His dad pulled his mom into his arms and kissed her, and Dare walked away leaving them alone. Seeing his family happy and together made him realize that he couldn't let anything stop him from telling Melody how he felt.

Melody's mom and brother were both sitting on the porch chatting when she arrived. Martha's Vineyard was made for summer, Melody thought. Normally she didn't spend a lot of time here because she'd taken classes over the summer while she was in college and then last year she'd been working as a paid intern in New York. For the first time in her life, Melody realized she wasn't thinking about work or getting back to the office. Everything had changed last night with Dare and she realized that she liked the new feeling.

She waved at them as she got out of the car and went to sit next to them. Her mom reached over and ruffled her hair and Ben offered her a can of cream soda from the cooler next to his chair. She took one.

"Okay, what's going on?" her mom asked. "It's not like you to take the weekend off."

She smiled. "Well, I met a guy and I think I'm finally getting a life."

"Good. It's about time," Ben said.

She gave her brother the finger and then blew him a kiss.

"Who is he?" her mom asked. "Do we know him? Do you work with him? Workplace romances never work out."

"Says the woman who married her subordinate," her dad said, coming out to join them.

Melody and Ben laughed.

"Hush, Stan, we were different," her mom said.

"So is she, Bebe," Stan said. "So you're dating someone?"

"Yes," she said.

Everyone was looking at her, waiting for her to drop his name, and she realized she was nervous. But if she was going to date Dare, she had to let her family know. And it was more than dating; Melody knew that now. She loved him and she wanted more than clandestine sexual encounters with him.

"Um, it's Dare Bisset."

"The senator?" Bebe asked.

"Of the Bissets?" Stan asked.

"Go, girl!" Ben said.

"Thanks, Ben. And yes to the other questions. We met when I snuck into that wedding reception earlier this summer and just hit it off. We've been seeing each other on the down low, since I work for a lobbyist and he's a senator, and we didn't want to ruffle any feathers, but it's getting serious…so I wanted you guys to know."

"How serious?" her dad asked.

"I'm going to meet his family tomorrow on Nantucket. And I'm going to let my boss know about the relationship and ask to be moved to another project that doesn't put me in direct conflict with Dare."

"Good. It's always better to be up-front. But you should also be prepared in case your boss decides to terminate your employment. It's a possibility here." Her father wasn't one to mince words.

"I am," she said. And she was. She'd had time last night after she'd talked to Dare and again this morning while she was on the ferry to Martha's Vineyard to really explore different possibilities. She had a few ideas; one of them was to become a legal counsel for families like Blanche's, who needed help getting their message to the right people in Congress.

"I'm glad to hear that," her dad said.

"So, what's he like?" her mom asked. "I mean, his family is über-rich and they're always hosting famous people and doing charity events. It seems like you two wouldn't have much in common, given your age difference."

"He's not what you'd expect. Of course, he has the trappings of wealth but he's a really nice guy with a big heart. He has a Saint Bernard named Bailey and after he runs he gives him ice cream. He's smart and considerate. You'll like him, Mom."

"He sounds like a saint," Ben said. "I think you might be exaggerating."

"I'm not," Melody said, but feeling so full of love for Dare it was hard to think of any flaws he had. Of course, he had been really mad when he'd found out she'd played him and she knew he had a temper, but that was Dare the senator and not Dare her boyfriend.

"Good, then. I'm glad you're dating someone. I think we all were afraid you'd never do anything but work," Ben said.

"You're such a brat. Dad, why didn't you spank him more when he was younger?" Melody teased.

"You know we don't believe in corporal punishment, which is probably a good thing because you were a bit cheeky, too," Dad said.

They sat around laughing and joking and Melody realized that finding Dare had added an element to her life that she hadn't realized she'd been missing. She'd always been so focused on the external and making her big goals happen as fast as she could that she'd never taken the time to just chill with her family.

Her phone pinged and she glanced down to see it was a text from Dare.

Miss you. Hope you are safely with your family and having fun.

She quickly typed, I am. Miss you too. :*

He sent the kiss emoji back and she put her phone down, looking up to see her family watching her.

"You're in love with him, aren't you?" her mom asked.

"I am."

Her mom nodded at her, looking a bit concerned. Her dad just smiled.

"It's about time," her dad said.

But it was her mom's concern that made her worry. Did she think that Dare was out of her league? Was she being foolish without realizing it? She wasn't sure. The only thing she did know was that there was no way she'd be able to change her feelings for him even if she wanted to.

Which wasn't the best feeling in the world.

Dare's grandmother's house was more impressive than Melody had expected it to be. The driveway was long and had a lot of cars parked in it. A butler answered the door offering to take her bag and asking what she wanted to drink.

"Just water," she said.

"Very well. If you change your mind later let me know. Follow me to the veranda where the family is gathered. I'm Michael, by the way."

"Melody Conner," she said.

"Nice to meet you," he said as he led the way down a hall lined with photos of Dare's immediate family and some older ones that she assumed were his ancestors. The flooring was hardwood with a thick beautifully designed rug that felt soft under her feet.

Michael opened the door to the rear porch and gestured for her to step through. As soon as she did all conversation stopped and it felt like every one of Dare's family members turned to look at her. She wished she'd done something other than put her hair in a ponytail. She was still wearing a pair of white denim shorts and a polo shirt. So not too fancy.

"Melody, I'm so glad you're here," Dare said, coming over to her side and hugging her. "I'm sure you remember my mom and dad."

"I do. It's nice to see you both again, Mr. and Mrs. Bisset."

They both smiled warmly at her. "We're so glad you could join us."

"I know you met Zac. That's Iris sitting next to him. Then Logan and Quinn and Leo and Danni," Dare said. "Nick and Adler will be back in a bit. They ran to pick up his family at the ferry."

There were so many people that Melody felt a bit overwhelmed. On top of that, to be in love with Dare was making her more nervous than she'd ever been before.

She took a seat on a sofa next to Dare. Her phone vibrated in her pocket and she gratefully took it out to look at it, needing an escape.

But when she read the news alert, she wasn't sure she'd read it correctly.

Senator Dare Bisset caught in love tryst with lobbyist Melody Conner just days before the Senate is to vote on his latest legislation.

Oh. Damn.

Suddenly everyone's phones were buzzing in the room.

"This isn't good."

"No, it's not," Dare agreed.

"I have to call Johnny before this goes any further," she said. "Please excuse me."

Dare just nodded and stood up as she left the veranda.

Melody called Johnny's direct line and he answered on the first ring.

"Conner. This doesn't look good. I'm afraid we are going to have a meeting when you get back to DC."

"It's not what the article says. We started out as friends, Johnny. I didn't mean to let it become more. I haven't done anything that would compromise my work ethics or my commitment to our lobbying."

"We'll talk when you're back in town. Aubrey sent some notes over suggesting that you tried to sway a witness to go and talk to Bisset. Is that true?"

"No. I wouldn't do that," Melody said.

"It doesn't look good. I'm going to discuss this

with the team, but I think your future with Rose-mond group might be over."

"I'll respect your wishes, but I didn't do those things. Or leak this story," she said.

"But who did? It's not like you have enemies, but Bisset does. See what you can find out. I'll give you until Monday to change my mind."

She hung up with her boss and then opened the news article on her phone. She skimmed it but then read it more closely. The article actually made it sound as if she'd been stirring things up for Dare and making the witnesses speak out more harshly about him. Was Aubrey trying to make her look bad at work and in her relationship? But why would she leak this information? It wasn't as if she was going to get a bigger role at Rosemond Group because of this. Maybe Aubrey thought things would be easier with Melody out of the way, but by leaking to the press, she'd harmed the firm and Johnny wouldn't just let that go.

She texted Aubrey.

Did you talk to the press about me and Bisset?

The answer was almost immediate. Yes. You can't play both sides.

That's unfair. I'm not going to let you get away with this.

Too late. I didn't say anything that wasn't true.

You told JR that I tried to influence the witnesses' statements. That's a lie.

Who's going to believe you now?

Melody wanted to scream. She pocketed her phone and then went to find Dare.

But he came into the hallway.

"Why would you say that my office told a single mom that her child's illness wasn't important?"

"I didn't say that."

"The press release came from your office."

"I have no need to make up stories about you, Dare. The press release I helped draft was sharing the story of Blanche—a woman I met and interviewed along with Aubrey. We will get the votes without me doing that. Aubrey made the adjustments."

"Did you just deny to Johnny that we were dating?" he asked her sharply.

"No. Of course not. I am not going to lie about us. I made it clear that I could never compromise my job or my own ethics." She shook her head in frustration. "We can keep going back and forth or you can trust me," she said.

He stood there watching her, and she knew that he was on the defensive. Surely he knew her well enough to see she wouldn't defame him?

"Dare, this is me."

He gave her a sarcastic look. "Yeah. The woman who crashed a wedding to get close to me and used the information she gathered to try to block a bill.

Your kind will do anything to get ahead. Including leaking stories about me—about us—to the press."

"I already told you I didn't do that. I screwed up and I'm pretty sure Johnny's going to fire me over this," she said.

"Karma."

She shook her head. She wanted to talk things through, but he wasn't in the mood and he was making her mad. She couldn't deny things she'd done in the past, but she'd changed and she'd thought they'd both realized that.

"Yeah, maybe it is," she said, turning and walking away.

Dare let her leave, which told her more than she wanted it to. She got as far as the foyer, where the butler was waiting with her bag and no friendly smile and she forced herself to take it calmly.

"Thanks. I'll wait outside for my Uber."

Fifteen

Dare went back in to find his entire family watching him. He stood there for a minute, realizing that he hated being the center of this kind of attention. It brought him immediately back to his childhood when he'd heard his parents fighting and they'd quiet down when he walked into the room.

It was that kind of moment for him. He was tense, angry that he hadn't seen the truth about Melody. No one said a word until Logan got up and walked over to him, clapping him on the shoulder.

"Want a drink?"

Drink? No, he wanted to yell or punch someone. He wanted a fight so he could get rid of this anger, but that wasn't going to happen with his grandmother sitting there and all these women in the room. He would be the good guy he always was. "Yes. Whiskey neat."

"On it," Logan said, not ringing the bell for Michael but going to fix the drink himself.

Quinn was typing rapidly on her smartphone and then held her finger up to him. "I think there is more to this story than we realized."

"What more could there be?"

Dear God. He hoped his office really hadn't turned a woman and her child away as coldly as that article had made it sound. That was the kind of action his predecessor had been known for. It was exactly the type that Dare had gotten into politics to stop. He pulled his own phone out and texted Cami the woman's name and asked her to check their calendar and the security logs for both offices to see if she'd been there. He continued typing:

Get me her number so I can find her and fix this.

Cami got back to him right away. I will. I don't think she came to either office but I'm on it.

Thank you.

You okay?

Dare sent her the thumbs-up emoji and put down his phone.

"I wonder if this is more of someone just trying to

stir the pot since our name has been in the tabloids so much lately," Leo said.

"Yeah, it was," Dare said. "According to the article Melody is the one who gave them the information, which she denied, of course."

"That's not what my sources are telling me," Quinn said. "The source sent the photo of you two kissing along with the release. There is no way that Melody took that photo."

He found the article again on his phone and the photo where he'd kissed her. She definitely hadn't taken it and he remembered that night on the yacht. She'd pushed for them to be open about their relationship to continue it. Why would she do that if she was planning to sell her story?

Damn.

"Did you get a name?"

"Not yet, but I will," Quinn said.

"I'll be back. Text me when you have it," Dare said, heading for the door and running into Logan, who was returning with a drinks tray.

"Hey."

"I screwed up. I have to go," Dare said. He sprinted down the hall, hoping that he'd be able to catch Melody before she left.

But he was too late. He got to the front door just in time to watch the taillights of the Uber she'd called pull out of the driveway.

He quickly texted her.

I screwed up. We were set up by someone else.

You did, was the blistering response. It's that co-worker who saw us in Boston.

Come back. I can fix this.

You can't. You'd have to trust me and we both know you never will.

Dare typed out Please but then deleted it. Could he beg her to come back? Should he? How would he know if he could trust her? Sure, it was easy this time but his gut went straight to suspecting her and he knew he had to figure out how to convince her—and himself—that he could trust her.

Melody texted again while he was trying to figure out what to do.

Just leave this for now. See you around.

No. I can't. Please come back and let's talk this out.

I have to try to fix this with my boss. And you hurt me. I'm not ready to forgive you.

Dare hadn't realized that he needed her to forgive him until that moment. He hit the phone icon at the top of their text conversation and it started ringing, but he wasn't sure she'd answer.

"What?" she answered.

"I'm sorry."

"Fine."

"No, it's not fine. I should have done more than skim the article and react to it. I have no excuse for that. But when I saw the headline I remembered how we met in DC, and then you showing up with Johnny—"

"I know," she said. "It looked bad."

"It did, but I should have trusted you."

"Yes, you should have," she said.

He heard the sound of the ferry horn and knew she was leaving and his gut said if he didn't fix things with her now it would be too late.

"Don't get on the ferry. Stay and talk this through with me."

"Why? We both knew this was going to be a hard relationship to figure out but also that maybe we shouldn't be together. Doesn't this seem like a nudge to stop it now?"

"For you, maybe. But I care about you, Melody. I didn't just bring you home for kicks. I want you to be a part of my life and my family."

"Oh, Dare. I want that, too," she said.

"Wait for me. I'll come to the ferry terminal. I want to talk in person."

There was a long silence on the phone and he held his breath, hoping she'd agree. But if she said no, then he'd have the answer. He'd know that it wasn't politics or her career keeping them apart.

"I will," she said. "I'm sitting on one of the benches that face the water. Come and find me."

He wasted no time, getting into his Gran's '69 Camaro and going after the woman he loved and didn't want to let slip away.

Humiliated and angry but hopeful, too, Melody stood near the ferry terminal waiting for Dare to arrive.

He should have trusted her. She got why he didn't. Knew that she'd sown the seeds of doubt with the way they'd met and how she'd behaved.

But he should have known her better now. Should have been able to tell that she loved him and would never betray him that way. But maybe he couldn't see that. And perhaps he didn't feel the same way about her as she did about him.

Whatever.

Except not whatever. She wanted to cry but refused to do that while she was standing there waiting for him. She put on her sunglasses and texted her mom to say she was coming back tonight. Her mom immediately called her back.

"Honey, we saw the article. How can we help?" she asked.

"How did you see it?" Did everyone know?

"Ben showed us. Dad is already on the phone with the lawyer to see what we can do—"

"Mom, stop. That is me kissing Dare, as you

know, and I did write a press release that was meant to be sent out. Part of the article is what I wrote."

"Only part of it?" her mom asked.

"Yes. In fact, Mom, let me call you back." She realized that she'd sent her version of the press release to Constance. So she'd have the copy of what Melody had sent.

"Okay, honey. We love you."

She hung up and dialed Johnny's number. She knew that it was Aubrey who'd leaked the photo and she thought she could prove that Aubrey had altered the press release.

"Conner. Glad you called. We found some discrepancies between the press release you sent Constance yesterday and the one that was leaked to the press. Constance is on the phone with Senator Bisset's office right now. We are trying to get to the bottom of this. We are thinking of firing the person responsible for the leak."

Firing her? Melody felt a twinge of guilt. She knew that Aubrey had made her own choices, which could lead to her losing her job, but at the same time, Melody had crashed a wedding to get the scoop on her coworkers, had she unconsciously set a tone in the office of doing whatever was necessary to get ahead.

"Was it Aubrey, sir?"

"Yes, it was."

"I don't think she should be fired. I was the one who had the inappropriate relationship, which might have led her to think I wouldn't treat our team fairly and though she leaked information from our office, I'm sure she wouldn't do it again."

Johnny leaned back in his chair and stared at her across the expanse of his desk. "I'm listening."

"It's just that everyone makes mistakes. Sir, I know Aubrey well enough to know she's learned from this. I doubt she'd do it again."

"Do you think the two of you can work together and make this right?" Melody wasn't sure but she knew she'd do whatever she could.

"I'll do whatever I can to fix this."

"I know you will. This makes us look bad and I don't play the game like this. We use facts to sway congressmen to our side, not gossip and lies."

"Yes, sir. I do get the feeling that there is probably some common ground for you to take to subcommittee," she said.

"I do, too. I like you, Conner. But we are going to have to figure out if you can continue working for me in a different capacity," Johnny said.

"I'd like that, too. But I can't work on the campaign to block Senator Bisset's bill."

"Definitely not," he said. "Constance will be emailing you later to collect further information from you. Are we good?"

Were they good? She thought they were. She liked working for Johnny and he'd immediately come clean with her when the facts had been found. "Yes."

"Good. I really like your work ethic and want you on my team."

"Me, too."

She hung up with Johnny and sat on the bench facing the ocean, watching the boats and trying to figure out what she was going to say when Dare got here. She'd never allowed her emotions to have such control over her life before and she couldn't help feeling like it was a mistake. Being vulnerable left her scared and not sure what to do next.

She wanted to just go home to her parents and let them take care of her while she licked her wounds. But Dare had offered her a chance of hope. The hope that maybe they could work things out.

Could they?

How would she know until they were tested again?

"Hey."

She turned to see him standing next to her.

"Hey."

"Can I sit down?" he asked. "Or do you want to walk and talk?"

She glanced around, noticing there tourists nearby. And given that the Bissets had been in the headlines all summer, people were looking at them.

"Walk," she said, standing up.

He fell into step beside her as she led the way down to the beach.

"So, I'm sorry," he said.

"I know."

"Melody, it's been a long time since I cared about

someone the way I do for you," he said. "It's scary to admit but you make me vulnerable."

She stopped walking, pushing her sunglasses up on her head. "You do the same for me. I've never let something like this interfere with my goals for my life and my career before."

"Something like this?" he asked, quirking one eyebrow at her.

"An affair." She was afraid to say anything else.

"I thought we agreed this was more than an affair," he said.

"That was before you kicked me out of your grandmother's house."

He nodded. "You're not going to be able to forgive me, are you?"

"Can you forgive me for deceiving you when we met? To me it seems like this is really two sides of the same coin. We have to both go all-in or there is no point in us being together."

She held her breath, waiting to see what he would say. And he reached for her, drawing her into his arms. He leaned in close so that he was whispering in her ear.

"I love you, Melody. I've been afraid to admit that to myself but it's true. When I saw that headline and then read the article, it stung. Because I wondered how I could have fallen for your charms and not seen the truth about you." He lifted his head and stared down into her eyes. "But I did see the truth. You wouldn't betray me and I know that. I know you for an honest woman who isn't afraid to go after an opportunity when she sees it but also would never hurt someone she cares for."

"Oh, Dare. Yes. That is me. I love you, too. I've never said that to a man before and when you—"

"I'm sorry."

"You don't have to say it again. Let's never do that again."

"Agreed."

Epilogue

One year later

"Busted."

Melody Conner-Bisset arched one eyebrow at the tall, dark, handsome man who had put a ring on her finger earlier that evening. He leaned in to block her view of the rest of the crowd at their wedding reception.

The scandal that had revealed their relationship had made them both stronger as a couple. Dare had modified his bill to include funding for research that would help families like Blanche's as well as a low fixed price prescription program that would benefit all Americans.

Melody had transitioned into working on other research projects in a role that didn't involve meeting with members of congress.

"You caught me. So now what?" she asked.

"I'm never letting you go," he said.

The last year had been a good one. Melody had learned that having a partner by her side made her stronger. Made her happier.

"Son, we need you," August called him.

Melody watched Dare go over to his father. The Bisset men were up to something. Juliette Bisset slipped her arm around Melody's shoulder as she came over to her side.

"This wedding was perfect," Juliette said.

"Almost as nice as the vow renewal you and August had in Italy on Lake Garda," she said.

"That was special. I never would have guessed we'd be back on Nantucket for another wedding and that the family would still be together," Juliette admitted.

"Me, neither," Adler Williams said. "To be honest, Uncle Auggie really has changed and I'm glad to see all of that scandal is behind us."

"Hush," Quinn said. "Scandal is what my industry thrives on. Your wedding was the highest-rated reality TV event last year."

Logan had eloped with Quinn just before Christmas so she and Melody were now sisters-in-law. Leo and Danni had had a very private wedding in the Hamptons in March, which had been lovely.

"It's nice to have some quiet," Danni said.

"I wish I had some," Marielle said as she came up next to them holding her tiny baby girl. Delia was six months old. Mari and Inigo had married during Inigo's break from Formula One when Mari was hugely pregnant with their baby. They both admitted that as much as they adored her, she had a set of lungs on her and the only thing that quieted her down was Inigo driving her around their neighborhood while Mari sang "Baby Shark." Which had cracked up Mari's siblings.

Melody loved being a part of this family. Her parents had been in attendance at the vow renewal for August and Juliette and had become good friends with them.

Once Olivia Williams had taken over the joint venture between Nick and Logan, the families had started to become friends, which had been a shock to Melody and Dare.

She noticed her brother flirting with Olivia and Melody secretly thought they'd make a good couple.

"Ladies and gentleman, thank you for coming to celebrate our wedding with us. I hope you will indulge the men in my family while we try to show our woman how we feel."

All of them looked at each other, waiting for whatever was coming next. Toby Osborn came onto the stage with his guitar and started playing "This Will Be An Everlasting Love." August, Dare, Logan, Leo,

Inigo and Nick all came onto the stage and sang for all they were worth.

Melody fell a little bit more in love with Dare at that moment. This day had been the perfect beginning for the rest of her life, she thought.

When the song was over, Dare came back to her and pulled her into his arms.

"I love you, Mrs. Bisset."

"And I love you, Mr. Bisset."

* * * * *

Don't miss a single book in the
Destination Wedding series by USA TODAY
bestselling author Katherine Garbera!

Her One Night Proposal
The Wedding Dare
The One from the Wedding
Secrets of a Wedding Crasher

Available from Harlequin Desire.

#2875 BOYFRIEND LESSONS
Texas Cattleman's Club: Ranchers and Rivals
by Sophia Singh Sasson
Ready to break out of her shell, shy heiress Caitlyn Lattimore needs
the help of handsome businessman Dev Mallik to sharpen her dating
skills. Soon, fake dates lead to steamy nights. But can this burgeoning
relationship survive their complicated histories?

#2876 THE SECRET HEIR RETURNS
Dynasties: DNA Dilemma • by Joss Wood
Secret heir Sutton Marchant has no desire to connect with his birth
family or anyone else. But when he travels to accept his inheritance, he
can't ignore his attraction to innkeeper Lowrie Lewis. Can he put the
past behind him to secure his future?

#2877 ROCKY MOUNTAIN RIVALS
Return to Catamount • by Joanne Rock
Fleur Barclay, his brother's ex, should be off-limits to successful rancher
Drake Alexander, especially since they've always despised one another.
But when Fleur arrives back in their hometown, there's a spark neither
can ignore, no matter how much they try...

#2878 A GAME BETWEEN FRIENDS
Locketts of Tuxedo Park • by Yahrah St. John
After learning he'll never play again, football star Xavier Lockett finds
solace in the arms of singer Porscha Childs, until a misunderstanding
tears them apart. When they meet again, the heat is still there. But they
might lose each other once more if they can't resolve their mistakes...

#2879 MILLION-DOLLAR CONSEQUENCES
The Dunn Brothers • by Jessica Lemmon
Actor Isaac Dunn needs a date to avoid scandal, and his agent's sister,
Meghan Squire, is perfect. But pretending leads to one real night...
and a baby on the way. Will this convenient arrangement withstand the
consequences—and the sparks—between them?

#2880 CORNER OFFICE CONFESSIONS
The Kane Heirs • by Cynthia St. Aubin
To oust his twin brother from the family company, CEO Samuel Kane
sets him up to break the company's cardinal rule—no workplace
relationships. But it's *Samuel* who finds himself tempted when
Arlie Banks awakes a passion that could cost him everything...

Maxton eyed Teagan and asked, "Isn't there something I didn't get to see?"

She smiled. "If you mean my bedroom, you gotta earn it, playboy."

"Sounds like a challenge," he quipped.

She shook her head. "No. More of a requirement."

He laughed, then gently dragged the tip of his index finger along her jawline. "You're going to make me work for this. I just know it."

Her answer was a sultry smile. "We'll just have to see what happens."

"Truth is, I really don't have the time for a relationship right now."

If she took offense at his statement, she didn't show it. "Neither do I."

"So, what are we doing here?"

She shrugged. "A fling? A dalliance? I don't think it really matters what we call it, so long as we both understand what it is…and what it isn't."

Their gazes met and held, and the sparkle of mischief in her eyes threatened to do him in. "Enlighten me, Teagan. What will we be doing, exactly?"

"We hang out…have a little fun. No strings, no commitments. And, above all, we don't let this thing interfere with our work or our lives." She pressed her open palm against his chest. "That is, if you think you can handle it."

"Seems reasonable." *I like this approach. Seems like we're on one accord.*

Her smile deepened. "Tomorrow is my only other free day for a while. Why don't you meet me at the Creamery, right near Piedmont Park? Say around seven?"

"I'll be there." He wanted to kiss her but couldn't read her thoughts on the matter. So he grazed his fingertip over her soft glossy lips instead.

"See you then," she whispered.

Satisfied, he opened the front door and stepped out into the afternoon sunshine.

Don't miss what happens next in…
After Hours Temptation
by Kianna Alexander.

Available June 2022 wherever
Harlequin Desire books and ebooks are sold.

Harlequin.com